Henri Mortimer

We Were Only Strawberry Picking

Henrietta Defreitas

**Grosvenor House
Publishing Limited**

This book is published by
Grosvenor House Publishing Ltd
28-30 High Street, Guildford, Surrey, GU1 3EL.
www.grosvenorhousepublishing.co.uk

A CIP record for this book
is available from the British Library

ISBN 978-1-78148-886-7

This is the third book of a series written
By Henrietta Defreitas

Chapters

CHAPTER ONE

The Meerville
Strawberry Fields

It was another glorious weekend as Henratty peered through the gleaming window panes, immersed by the rays of sunlight beaming through. She was certainly bored, as she breathed heavily on the recently polished glass and began to scribble her name. She watched the letters disappear one by one and then repeated the process several times. Her mother, Mama Mortimer, was doing the weekly cleaning, so she was not in the best of moods. Henratty desperately wanted to go outside and play with her younger sister, Lyndi Lou, but she was dubious about asking her mother right now. She had to see when she was in a better mood and then ask.

Henratty was still reminiscing about playtime until the sudden clanking of saucepans and cutlery tumbling to the ground had startled her, as she stopped daydreaming. She knew instantly that her mother had accidentally dropped these items in a rush to wash up. This was the only household chore Mama Mortimer hated the most and could never wait for the task to be over with, but generally cleaning never was her strong point! If there was a record for the fastest washer-upper in Meerville Town, she had no doubt that her mother would be the outright winner, providing she managed to hang onto the dishes in the first place!

Whilst Mama Mortimer was muttering to herself, no doubt frustrated, as she continued to chase the runaway cutlery along the kitchen floor, Henratty had now turned her attention to Lyndi Lou as she closely watched her finish eating her breakfast so elegantly. She really did take a long time eating her food, she was a proper little madam and most things had to be precise! Henratty then had this awful thought that if it were Jack Brian instead, not only would he have finished his food in seconds, but he would also have licked off every morsel he could find on his plate. The word "gross" came to mind, but thank goodness Jack was just a friend, she sighed with relief.

Having taken her plate to Mama Mortimer to wash up, Lyndi Lou rushed over excitedly, as she said to Henratty, 'Well, what shall we do today?'

'I'm not sure but it's a beautiful day, so let's do something outside and to be honest, I think we've had enough of staying in,' grumbled Henratty, as she placed one hand on her chin and began tapping with the other on the slightly worn but well veneered dining table, whilst she contemplated what they were going to do.

Lyndi Lou was staring hard at Henratty, as she waited patiently for her to come up with something more adventurous than *hide and seek*! Also her continuous tapping was annoying Lyndi Lou somewhat who had been biting her tongue the whole time, and now on the verge of saying something. However, before she could say a word, Henratty had stopped tapping and was smirking. Lyndi Lou knew then that her sister had come up with something exciting for playtime.

'I have a great idea, it's strawberry season so why don't we grab our baskets and go strawberry picking. We can also give some to Jack and Oscar to see if they can get Mama Katie to make her delicious strawberry tart that we all love,' decided Henratty.

'That's a brilliant suggestion, why didn't I think of that, you know how much I love strawberries,' Lyndi Lou pronounced happily. She decided she would need to change into her favourite pink dress because it was so hot, as she darted upstairs and chuckled, *'Pretty in pink that's me!'*

Now, all Henratty had to do was to convince their mother to let them go strawberry picking, as she headed towards the kitchen apprehensively, where Mama Mortimer was still washing up and still wittering to herself.

* * *

Having spent an excessive amount of time pampering herself, Lyndi Lou had returned even more elated, as Henratty was explaining to Mama Mortimer where they were going.

'Just make sure you do what the attendant says and I expect you both back here well before lunchtime,' Mama Mortimer said more sternly than usual, as she was fully aware that they had had ample playtime recently, in fact, far too much. However, they just loved every minute of their playtime and were thankful that they were being allowed out. Deep down they knew they should be catching up with homework, but there was always tomorrow!

Henratty had cleverly worked out that Mama Mortimer would let them out once she mentioned they were picking strawberries so that they could get Jack and Oscar to ask their mother, Mama Katie, to make her lovely strawberry tart. She had also noticed her mother give a broad smile when she mentioned why they were going strawberry picking. In Henratty's eyes, this was a sure sign that she approved, not to mention the fact she had stopped giving them a lecture on the copious amount of playtime they had had already.

Finally, Henratty and Lyndi Lou briskly made their way to the front door having listened intently to everything their mother had said, and all they could think about was strawberry picking! Henratty pulled frantically on the front door, as she needed to quickly escape before their mother changed her mind, and as it opened, they were greeted by the strong rays of sunshine – they both squinted and shielded their eyes from the intense sunlight with the palms of their hands. It was extremely hot and sticky, but they did not care, they just wanted to get to those strawberry fields and nothing was going to stop them. However, before the door could shut firmly, it was suddenly yanked open by Mama Mortimer. Henratty's heart sank, she hoped that her mother had not changed her mind as she suspected only a couple of seconds ago, but Mama Mortimer was just being extra cautious and thinking of the welfare of her meerkats.

'Just watch that sun you two, I don't want you both coming home sunburnt to a crisp,' Mama Mortimer said, as she gave the sunblock to Henratty with a look on her face that meant wear this or else … They both hated the smell and the feel of the lotion on their skin but they always wore it reluctantly as they knew it did stop them from burning. Also if they came back sunburnt, they knew that their parents would definitely not let them play out again, as their mother had just inferred and all because they did not wear any sunblock, it just wasn't worth the risk!

'Thanks mama, don't worry we'll be extra careful ...' and off they went on their one mile trek to the strawberry fields, but not before Henratty insisted that they apply the sunblock as she had seen their mother peep through the curtains from the corner of her eye.

* * *

At last they had arrived at Meerville Strawberry Fields. The air smelt lovely and sweet as they paid the attendant and entered the enormous field brimming with juicy red strawberries. They could see a few other meerkats already in the fields but it was not that busy, luckily!

'Where shall we start then?' asked Lyndi Lou excitedly.

'How about over there, on the far left. No one seems to be picking strawberries there,' and off they trundled. However, as they got a little closer, Lyndi Lou had noticed the *No Trespassing Sign!*

'But, it says no strawberry picking in this area – look there's the Danger Sign,' as she pointed to the red notice. The colour "red" should have set alarm bells ringing, however, against her better judgement, Henratty had already decided that she was going to ignore this sign.

'Oh, I'm sure no one will notice. What could possibly harm us in there? It looks exactly the same as this field – see no difference apart from that warning sign.'

'I would say there is a big difference, as it's not just any sign, it says, "DANGER, NO TRESPASSING, AND

THOSE FOUND WILL BE PROSECUTED!" Mama will see red if she knew what you were about to do. Where are you going, Henratty?' demanded Lyndi Lou as she tugged on her sister's cape.

'Stop making a scene, otherwise we will get caught, and then we will be in trouble. Now please be quiet and follow me.' On that note, Lyndi Lou decided it was pointless discussing the danger sign anymore as she could tell that Henratty was determined to enter that field and there was nothing she could do to stop her.

Having scanned the surrounding area, when no one was looking, Henratty signalled for Lyndi Lou to move, in a crouched position, as they slipped through a gap in the fence and into the forbidden strawberry field. From this moment, there was no turning back and after just one look at those strawberries, they had both completely forgotten about the danger sign.

'Wow let's start over there, the strawberries look nice and juicy,' remarked Henratty and off they sprinted eagerly.

* * *

Meanwhile beneath them, and hundreds of feet down in the old mineshaft, Nora the bat had been awoken by the sudden tremor of the unstable ground above. She was hanging upside down in what she called her meditative state. Allowing the blood to rush to her head somehow made all her stress and anxiety disappear, but now this quiet period had been rudely interrupted and this had not happened for a long time, the last time being when two hedgehogs, Jasper and Nancy, fell down the mineshaft two years ago.

'What on earth was that?' she said aloud and then bellowed, 'Enoch, Enoch, ENOCH! Come quickly, I think we need to start preparing for some unwanted guests. If they continue to run around like that, there's only one place they're going to end up!'

'Oh, Batty, you could be right!'

'Enoch, how many times have I told you it's Nora, and not Batty?'

'I'm sorry, but as you're a bat, "Batty" is easier to remember than Nora – you know how forgetful I am ...'

'Look stop wasting time, forget about my name for now, this is far more important. I want you to go and warn the others if you can remember where they are, not to mention the conversation we have just had. Have you got that, Enoch?' asked Nora apprehensively.

'Of course I have, I know I'm forgetful but I'm not that dopey, am I?' as he wandered off trying to recite what Nora had told him to say and do, as she looked at him thinking, *Stupid mole, does he really want me to answer that?*

'I must warn the others to prepare for some unwanted guests,' Enoch continued to mumble until his silhouette had disappeared down the long dark tunnel with his voice becoming more and more faint until it was no more.

* * *

Back above the mineshaft in the forbidden field, Henratty and Lyndi Lou were painstakingly picking the best strawberries and placing them in the specially made containers in their baskets to avoid bruising.

'I just tried one – it's lovely, here you go, try this one,' as Henratty passed the strawberry to her sister.

'You're so right, but don't you think we have enough strawberries for today?' asked Lyndi Lou prudently.

'I guess you're right and like you said, we certainly don't want to get caught if we can help it, but we are definitely coming back tomorrow,' Henratty said adamantly. 'We need more than this if Mama Katie is going to make that special strawberry tart, and we can bring Oscar and Jack with us next time, after all Jack is the one that will probably eat most of the tart anyway,' as they giggled at the very thought of him stuffing his face with as many strawberries that he could fit in his mouth in one go.

They then scuttled back over to the permitted side of the field and by now everyone had left the entire strawberry fields as the attendant was about to lock up when they appeared behind him.

'Um – where were you two hiding? How come I did not see you? You're both very lucky as I was about to lock up. Next time, make sure you don't wander off too far, otherwise you could get locked in for sure.'

'We're terribly sorry, Sir, we promise we won't do it again,' responded Henratty as she smiled sweetly at the attendant.

On the way back, they decided they would take the long route home so they could stop by the Brians and show Jack and Oscar the gorgeous strawberries, to entice them to go strawberry picking tomorrow and instantly knew that once Jack had tasted these strawberries he would not resist, after all food came first!

* * *

An hour, later Henratty and Lyndi Lou were outside the Brians' doorway, as Mama Katie bellowed to Jack and Oscar that they had arrived, as they rushed out of their playroom into the hallway.

Jack was holding Oscar's MightyKats model but immediately dropped it on the floor as he saw Henratty's basket with the big ripe strawberries strategically sticking out of the basket. Her tactics had started to work.

'Strawberries,' Jack cried out, as he instinctively ran over and grabbed a handful from the basket, not even asking if he could try one.

'JACK!' screeched Oscar. 'Could you please mind what you do with my MightyKats model, you'll break it if you're not careful and papa will never buy me another one again. Is that what you want?'

'Of course not – I'm sorry,' as Jack forced another strawberry in his already filled mouth. 'So where did you get these lovely strawberries from?' as he continued to munch on them.

'Oh, Jack, we don't want to see what you're eating, thank you very much. Wherever did you get your manners from?' asked Henratty.

'I'm sorry, but they're so delicious ...' proclaimed Jack.

'If you come with us tomorrow, we promise to show you the secret place where we found these special strawberries, but we need to ask you a favour before we take you there,' said Henratty.

'Well, go on then what is it? I'm not going to promise anything until I know what you want,' enquired Jack intriguingly.

'All we want you to do is promise that you will ask Mama Katie to make that lovely strawberry tart, so we can take some home to our mother. Also, can you get us the recipe?'

'Done!' answered Jack without any hesitation.

'Are you sure? You know that's the one and only recipe that Mama Katie won't disclose to anyone. It's a secret that's been kept in the family for generations,' reminded Oscar vehemently.

'I'm sure,' responded Jack, as he had already worked out that he would just watch Mama Katie when she was making the strawberry tart and memorise most of the recipe. How would Henratty be able to tell whether he forgot a few ingredients or not, as long as he got most of it that would suffice!

Henratty looked at Jack a little unsure of his intentions, but she had no choice, as long as he got Mama Katie to make the strawberry tart that was the most important thing.

'Okay, that's settled then, we'll pass by tomorrow after lunch, that way it will stop you from eating all the strawberries if you have a full tummy,' quipped Henratty.

'I have a better idea, why don't we just meet you outside the entrance of Meerville Strawberry Fields around one thirty in the afternoon, that way you won't have to take the long route round,' suggested Jack.

'All right, we'll see you two tomorrow.'

* * *

They were now a clear distance away from the Brians' house and had walked in complete silence but Henratty could sense that Lyndi Lou did not seem herself.

'What's wrong, Lyndi Lou?' asked Henratty.

'Are you sure this is a good idea? When they see where the strawberries actually are, there is no way they will even enter that field,' declared Lyndi Lou.

'Trust me, when Jack sees the strawberries he is not going to be able to resist and once he goes, Oscar will naturally follow, so don't worry my plan will work,' said Henratty confidently.

'I just hope you know what you're doing, Henratty,' replied Lyndi Lou.

'Don't worry, I've got everything under control,' maintained Henratty. However, Lyndi Lou could not help feeling wary about trespassing, as she knew this could only spell trouble …

CHAPTER TWO

The Mineshaft

By now all the animals were gathered in Cooper's den. He was a rat with a chip on his shoulder, who had made it to the mine having escaped from Skylark (the unknown world in the sky ruled by these evil birds of prey called Larkans who had tried to take over The Land of Arkvale unsuccessfully many years ago). One of the Larkans' guards had not noticed that the latch on Cooper's door had not closed properly, even though it seemed like it had when visually checking, and so Cooper seized the opportunity to flee his chamber. He only had a matter of seconds to escape and his biggest regret was that he did not have time to let any of the other rats out. With literally no time to spare, all he could do was run and find a way out in the hope of coming back with help to rescue the other animals. He met Nora on the way who happened to have escaped at the same time, but the less said about Skylark, the better.

Cooper tried to pretend that Skylark did not exist, as the memories were too painful, but how could he, knowing the secret Nora and he kept for the sake of not only Meerville but the whole of Arkvale. This should have been a distant memory as this happened some thirty years ago, but as long as Skylark existed, Cooper could never forget and just lived day by day in the hope that the Larkans never succeeded in ruling Arkvale.

Cooper was now staring at Nora, as he got back to exactly why all the other mine inhabitants were gathered in his dormitory.

'So, what are we going to do about the intruders?'

'For the moment, nothing,' Nora proclaimed.

'Nothing, what do you mean nothing?' demanded Cooper.

'Well, it would appear that our little visitors have gone for the day, but I suspect they will return tomorrow, having got away with picking strawberries in the forbidden field.'

'So if they return and end up in the mineshaft as we did, what is the plan of action?' Cooper asked openly to all the animals.

'Attack I say, attack ...' cried Alfonso, the rattlesnake.

'Why would we attack those poor creatures?' asked Poppy the worm.

'Is that what you had planned for me, were you going to get Enoch to eat me?'

'Why on earth would I want to eat something as tasteless as you, Poppy?' declared Enoch.

'How do you know I'm tasteless unless you have eaten worms before?'

'Ho ... ho ... ho, you're funny, Poppy – you know I've never eaten worms before. I just meant you probably would be tasteless to me and, no offence, I hardly think you would be very filling.'

'Saved by my tastelessness ...' chuckled Poppy.

'You do make me laugh so much, Poppy,' giggled Enoch.

'I think we've heard enough from you two, so can we now get back to talking seriously, as our happy habitat is in danger of being invaded and ruined by these unknown visitors,' stated Nora.

Poppy had noticed that Escargot the snail was fast asleep once more, as she announced, 'Before we start, could someone please wake up Escargot, he has fallen asleep again.'

'Escargot wake up,' yelled Alfonso, as Nancy tapped on his shell until slowly he recoiled out of his home – out popped his antennae and then the rest of his neck.

'Oh, terribly sorry, did I miss something?'

'Attack, attack, attack,' repeated Alfonso as a frightened Escargot retracted back into his shell.

'Why did you have to go and say "attack" – now you've scared the living daylights out of Escargot,' said Cooper.

'Oh, for goodness sake, come back out Escargot, I wasn't talking about attacking you, I meant we need to attack the intruders and not give them a chance to seize our home – who knows what danger we could be in if we befriend them?' suggested Alfonso.

'But they could be our hope of a way out of this dismal place,' deemed Enoch, as Cooper gave him a piercing look. *(Due to Enoch's deteriorating memory, he had forgotten that he could get out of the mine at anytime and that's why Cooper was staring at him.)*

'I don't think attack is the solution, I think slow and measured steps are required; I think we should capture them,' declared Cooper.

'Okay, capture is even better, then we can interrogate them and maybe I could scare them a little with my rattle to make sure they know we mean business,' Alfonso smirked excitedly.

'Oh, Alfonso, shut up please! You lost your rattle only recently and you are no way ready to shed your skin, so how can you rattle without a rattle?' noted Nora.

'Well, I forgot about that – what good is a rattlesnake without its rattle I say!' as all of the other animals began to laugh hysterically at what Alfonso had just expressed, even Nora smiled amusingly.

'The plan is tomorrow I will take first watch, with my echolocation it shouldn't take me too long to determine roughly where their point of entry will be. It's going to take them a while to get their bearings, meanwhile I will signal Enoch so he can come back and round up everyone else. From the amount of dust that came down following the disturbance above, it sounded like only two creatures, so I think we can handle them between us. For now, we need to conserve our strength and get some rest, as we have a big day ahead of us. Alfonso and Enoch, I suggest you go along the tunnels and turn out the lights to limit their visibility towards the centre of the mine and to give us some time to change our plan if need be. If you can do this first thing tomorrow that should suffice. Unless, there was anything else you all wished to discuss, I'm going back to continue my meditation and would prefer it if I was not disturbed at all. I need to clear my mind completely.'

'And I need to get some sleep,' moaned Cooper. 'So could you all vacate my room, now, and could someone please wake up Escargot again. Does he do anything else apart from sleep? Perhaps we should feed him to the visitors, as he is no use to us.' Out popped Escargot on that note, 'I heard that Cooper!'

'Oh, so you weren't sleeping after all? Are you really as lethargic as you make out or is it just that you're the laziest animal in Meerville? Sorry, I better rephrase that, more like the laziest on the planet!'

'Now, you two, this is not the time for petty squabbles, we need to remain united and show these intruders that we are able to live in harmony, despite our backgrounds. Also we have to for survival, so apologise to one another, if not move on. I'm leaving you all now, so stop squabbling and start preparing for tomorrow,' and off Nora went.

* * *

The next day, Jack and Oscar met Henratty and Lyndi Lou by the entrance of Meerville Strawberry Fields, as planned. They paid the attendant accordingly, at which point both Henratty and Lyndi Lou had noticed that fortunately it was a different attendant from yesterday, so they knew there was no chance they would be recognised, as they glanced at each other with a smug smile. The sweet aroma of the strawberries had already entered Jack's nasal cavity way before they had even reached the fields, and with his acute sense of smell that was not difficult.

'So, come on then, show us where you got those strawberries from, it's clearly not here as the last two strawberries I tried tasted awful, and you did say you had found them in a special place and it was a secret.'

'Jack, please try not to get too excited and anyway, if the strawberries are that bad, then how come you are still eating them relentlessly?' remarked Henratty.

'I guess I'm still hungry.'

'But surely you had lunch, as I told you to. I'm warning you, any strawberries that we pick when we get to that special field are strictly not for your consumption. Promise me, Jack! – I really want Mama Katie to make that strawberry tart and she needs the best strawberries!'

'All right then, I'll pick and eat my own strawberries and promise not to touch any of the ones in the baskets,' Jack agreed reluctantly.

'Now follow me and please be quiet, we don't want to draw attention to ourselves and make the attendant suspicious of our whereabouts or what we were really up to,' reminded Henratty, and so in single file, they quietly followed Henratty.

'It's over there in that field,' as she pointed beyond the fence. Oscar had now spotted the red notice, just as Lyndi Lou had done the previous day.

'But that sign says: *Danger – prohibited land and trespassers will be prosecuted!*'

'Just like I pointed out yesterday!' declared Lyndi Lou.

'Honestly, do you two have to do everything by the book? If there was any danger, would we honestly be here? There is nothing dangerous in that field unless you're scared of strawberries and anyway you tried them, Jack, and you're still here.' It suddenly dawned on him that they had not even tried the strawberries from this forbidden area and he was Henratty's "guinea pig"!

'How do you know it has not done me any harm, I ate loads yesterday and you guys had none?' protested Jack.

'Not strictly true, as we had one each and well, Jack, you're still here, breathing, talking and eating relentlessly, so I would say that's more than enough proof and from where I'm standing nothing has changed about you, not even the size of your stomach!' argued Henratty.

Jack had to admit that what Henratty had just mentioned was in fact true as he said, 'Okay, okay, I guess you're right.'

'So are we ready then?' There was a long pause, as Lyndi Lou's eyes shifted in Oscar's direction (she was certainly not comfortable with the idea of trespassing for the second time). He could see her awkwardness and he was not feeling that comfortable either, as they simultaneously looked at Jack, almost subliminally wanting him to make the decision for them. They did not want to get blamed for any potential mishaps especially when they were supposedly with their older and responsible siblings.

'Well, I'm all for it,' uttered Jack. 'I just want to get hold of those big, juicy strawberries and try them once more before I start picking them for Mama Katie's tart.'

'Right that's settled then, we're going in. Lyndi Lou, when the coast is clear, you can give us the signal and we can squeeze through the gap in the fence, as we did last time. However, Jack, you will have to climb over, so please don't get stuck, because that attendant will see you and game over, not to mention what our parents will do to us if we get caught – I'm sure you don't want that on your conscience … do you?' questioned Henratty, as she glared at Jack.

'Look, are you implying that I am too big to get through that gap in the fence, as I've had enough of your snide remarks for one day?' snapped Jack.

'Of course not, what I'm saying is the gap is too small, that's all!' replied Henratty, as she glanced sideways, a definite sign that she was not exactly telling the truth. Jack scratched his head for a moment as he tried to fathom out if Henratty was being sincere, it confused him, but the pungent smell of the irresistible strawberries had overpowered him once more as he concentrated on getting over the fence.

'Right then, I'll be as light as a feather, you'll see.' retaliated Jack. The rest of the meerkats stared at him for a few seconds trying to comprehend what he had said as, if anything, one would not describe Jack "as being light as a feather" but quite the opposite!

'Now what are you all staring at?' asked Jack with a bemused expression, as all the other meerkats suppressed their laughter by covering their mouths with both hands, desperately wanting to laugh but knowing the attendant would hear them. They could not risk making any sort of sound that would alert him to their exact whereabouts.

'Right, that's enough. Lyndi Lou, are we clear?' asked Henratty.

Yes, she signalled with the agreed hand motion – that was Henratty and Oscar through the fence safely. She had now signalled Jack to stay still as she could see the attendant coming towards her. She was holding her breath, as he was only a few yards away but by the *grace of the MightyKats*, an argument had broken out between two meerkats picking strawberries on the other side of the field as she saw the attendant make a quick dash in the direction of the commotion. Immediately she signalled Jack to climb the fence and indeed he did so in no time, after all he was reasonably fit, just a bit on the large size that's all. Seconds after, Lyndi Lou followed via the gap in the fence.

'Phew, that was pretty close but we made it,' Lyndi Lou beamed.

'Follow me,' Henratty commanded. They walked about thirty yards and there before them was the sight of the largest, bright red strawberries they had ever seen. Jack did not hesitate, he was the first to sprint toward the strawberries followed by the rest of them.

* * *

By this stage, Nora had been awoken by the thunderous sound below in the mineshaft, not to mention the flurry of earth coming down at a very fast pace caused by the unusual activity above.

'What was that? Enoch, you need to go and tell everyone that we have at the very least four visitors. I think they are going to be in for quite a shock soon if they continue stomping around up there. Go and tell the others to be ready for our little visitors. Well, go on then, stop gawping at me and be quick about it too, Enoch!'

'Yes, Nora, I'm on my way,' as he scurried through the pitch black tunnel. Instead of being scared, Enoch felt exhilarated at the thought of making new friends and having more company. He was already bored and needed a bit of stimulation and excitement, so maybe these creatures were just what he needed.

* * *

Back above the mineshaft, Henratty had given everyone *their marching orders* as to where they should pick the strawberries. She had given Jack and Oscar one of the baskets and off they went with very little protest from Jack, surprisingly. For this task, it was pretty obvious who was in charge ...

Whilst Henratty and Lyndi Lou were being rather selective, Oscar and Jack were not so picky.

'Jack, can you concentrate and stop eating all the strawberries, the good ones too, surely you've had enough now. Besides, if Henratty sees you she'll *have your guts for garters!*' Oscar said seriously.

'I suppose so,' as Jack shrugged his shoulders and got down to work.

Meanwhile Henratty had noticed that the area where they were picking strawberries was a bit thin on the ground and she could see some even bigger strawberries in a small area about twenty yards away.

'I'm going to try over there, but you can stay here for the time being,' Henratty said enthusiastically, as she grabbed one of the containers from the basket and ran over to the area she had spotted when suddenly, she screamed.

As Lyndi Lou turned around, her sister was clearly nowhere to be seen. She instinctively ran over and saw a gaping hole about two feet wide and all that remained of Henratty was her red beret lying on the ground.

Lyndi Lou picked up the beret and thought, *Now, we really are in trouble!* She could hear Henratty saying something but it was not very distinct, so she leaned over to take a closer peek in the hope she could hear more clearly. However, this was Lyndi Lou's biggest mistake as she suddenly lost her footing and fell, head first, into the hole as she screamed at the top of her voice. This time Jack did look up (he thought he had heard something earlier but typical Jack was too engrossed in the strawberries to even comprehend that it sounded like someone in danger). But, this time he was absolutely sure that someone was in trouble and that could only be Henratty or Lyndi Lou.

'Oscar, follow me I think that Henratty and Lyndi Lou might be in trouble,' and off they charged towards where he had heard the sound.

* * *

Henratty had just landed deep underground in the mineshaft and was still shouting for help when suddenly Lyndi Lou landed feet first in a slide position as she dug her heels into the earth to break her fall. Her pink dress was now a dusty pink having been covered in dirt. Unable to make out clearly who it was, as it was so dark in the tunnel, Henratty deduced it must be her sister judging by the high pitched scream she made as she landed.

'Are you all right, Lyndi Lou?'

'I think so, apart from the grazes on the back of my legs and elbows, I'll survive. What about you. What happened?'

'I'm okay! All I remember was running towards the area I saw the last of the strawberries and now I'm down here. The ground just suddenly gave way.'

'I guess we certainly now know why the danger sign is there!' remarked Lyndi Lou.

'I know, you're absolutely right, I should have listened to you the first time, mama and papa are going to be out of their minds with worry, not to mention the enormous trouble I have got everyone into! Did you tell Jack and Oscar to get help?'

'Er – Sorry, I didn't ... before I realised what you were saying, I peered over the gaping hole to see if

I could hear a little more clearly, but slipped and fell in too – not before grabbing your precious beret – here you go,' said Lyndi Lou, as she passed the beret to Henratty.

'Oh, thanks! I can see you managed to hold onto the basket of strawberries too!'

'Amazingly, don't know how I managed that as well. Where are we, it's so dark down here? Hopefully Jack and Oscar would have heard my loud scream and have probably notified the attendant to get help,' but Lyndi Lou was about to eat her words as suddenly there was one almighty thud. Whatever had landed was big as it blew up dirt in their faces, as they began to cough due to the choking dust that had engulfed them.

'Wow,' the voice said. 'That was such an adrenaline rush, I want to do it again, that has to be the longest slide I have ever been on.'

'JACK!' shouted Henratty loudly. 'What are you doing down here?' but before he could answer, there was another thud.

'Ouch!' Jack cried. 'That hurt.'

'Sorry,' apologised Oscar.

'OSCAR!' cried Henratty, as she gave her sister a sideways glance of despair.

'OH, NO, NOT OSCAR AS WELL!' Their hearts sunk as they were not just in big trouble, but they now realised they could be lost forever and their parents would be absolutely distraught.

'So, I take it you went for help before you both came down here?' demanded Henratty annoyingly.

'Er – I'm afraid not, I heard your scream and instinctively ran over and dived into the hole to come and rescue you,' said Jack.

'And how exactly have you rescued us, you've made everything a hundred times worse, as you do realise that nobody knows we are down here and we will never be found?' snapped Henratty.

'I'll find a way out,' retorted Jack. At this stage, Oscar and Lyndi Lou began to sob – they were naturally scared of the daunting prospects. Henratty then went over and gave them both a comforting hug.

'Look guys, Jack and I will get you out of here if it's the last thing we do, we'll work something out, I promise. Now, dry your eyes and let's get down to finding a way out – there just has to be one.'

Suddenly from nowhere, there was this intensity of light. Henratty, Lyndi Lou and Oscar immediately swung round towards the beaming light, as they shaded their eyes.

'Is that you, Jack?' asked Henratty.

'Of course it's me, who else would it be?'

'Where did you find that torch?' asked Henratty.

'I didn't find it, I just remembered that I had it in my army jacket the whole time. I told you I would rescue you and I now have the equipment to get you out of here!' declared Jack excitedly.

'Jack, it's a torch, try to be realistic, that is not going to get us out of here,' retaliated Henratty.

'But it's a start,' chirped Oscar defending his big brother. 'At least we can now see where we are going.'

'You're absolutely right, so let's get the basket of strawberries that Lyndi Lou brought down and it looks like you have done the same, Oscar. At least, we have something to eat for the time being,' remarked Henratty.

* * *

At the opposite end of the tunnel, unbeknown to them, Nora had been listening to what the meerkats were saying. She had figured out that there were indeed four creatures of unknown origin, they sounded young and fairly harmless from her analysis but she was not going to take any chances and would ensure that all the animals living in this mine were prepared. Still hanging upside down, Nora thought she would bide her time until the intruders got a little closer – she knew it was going to take them a good hour or maybe more to get to this side of the tunnel.

The unmistakable Enoch had returned!

'Well, Enoch, did you give the others the message as instructed?'

'Yes, Nora! Word for word!'

'I want you to go back and give them another message: tell everyone that I want them to assemble here. It's going to take Escargot a lifetime to get here, so he can stay at base, so too can Poppy and Nancy, but Cooper, Alfonso and Jasper can accompany you back here.'

'Cooper won't make it,' said a concerned Enoch.

'Of course he will, he's been cooped up in his little habitat for far too long, a change of scenery will do him good. The intruders won't be here for an hour or so, which will give him plenty of time to get here, half an hour at the most.' Have you got that, Enoch?'

'I think so!'

'Tell them it is crucial that they all come and that I have managed to work out we have four very young, and I'm pretty sure, very harmless creatures. The only thing I don't know is what type of species they are.'

'Will do, I can't wait to meet them!' and off he trundled once more to fetch the others. However, Enoch had not noticed that he had taken the wrong turning in the tunnel and was now heading towards the meerkats rather than base. That was the trouble with these tunnels they all looked alike and were so interlinked, once you lost your bearings, it could take you a very long while to get back to where you started and for Enoch even longer. He was thinking to himself, *I wonder who they are? Nora said they were young, I hope some of them were my age, they could even be like me! Oh, wouldn't it be just great to have another mole down here, real company at last – someone who truly understands me ...*

* * *

Jack shone the torch above them – they could see that they had fallen hundreds of feet underground. He then aimed the torch along the tunnel – visibility was still poor as they realised they were in one very long tunnel.

'So what should we do?' asked Henrattty.

'Well, for a start, we need to get moving, as this torch has a short battery life and I really don't know how long it is going to last, so the sooner we get going the sooner we'll get out of here!'

'Jack, you're absolutely right and may I say thank goodness you wore that jacket. What did I call it last time? "A ridiculous outfit" I seem to remember. Well, I apologise, as it could well be our saving grace at the moment. What else have you got in those pockets?' Henratty demanded.

'Let me see – hold this, Oscar,' as he passed over the torch. 'I have my two catapults, lots of string, my binoculars, a watch with a compass, my tank of water, a tiny shovel, metal detector, bonbons – my favourite sweets, a whistle, pen and paper. Oh, and papa's foghorn!'

'I think we've heard enough. Dust yourself off everybody and let's get moving. I suggest that we hold hands in a single file due to the poor visibility and that way we won't get separated. So I'll go first – Jack, pass me the torch,' and on they marched as Henratty led the way.

'Where do you think we are?' asked Lyndi Lou as they came upon some old tracks.

'I think we are in some sort of mine judging by these tracks. I do recall Papa Mortimer mentioning something a long time ago when he was giving us a history lesson on Meerville Town. However, I was not paying much attention but I think he said this mine had been closed some thirty years ago. I guess we're the only ones down here now ... there must be a way out. There must be a lift that would have taken the workers and cargo to the top of the mine, above ground, and I think that's what we need to find,' surmised Henratty. Jack had now got out his shovel and was scraping the side of the wall.

'What exactly are you playing at?' asked Henratty.

'I'm looking for diamonds,' Jack responded excitedly.

'Don't be so silly, if there were diamonds down here, don't you think the whole of Meerville would know about it?' deduced Henratty.

'Maybe they do, but they just couldn't find the right area to dig, as look, we have come to the end of this tunnel and there are four other tunnels to choose from. It's like a maze down here. I know there is treasure down here and I'm going to find it,' Jack proclaimed confidently.

'Will you please pay attention, Jack, and stop thinking that everything is an adventure.'

'Oh, Henratty, do you remember our last conversation regarding "adventure" at Oscar's birthday?'

'Please don't remind me, besides that's different, this is for real and we need to be responsible as we have Lyndi Lou and Oscar to think of.'

'I know that but we can still have fun!'

'Jack, this is no picnic, we could be in serious danger – who knows what's lurking down one of these tunnels? For all we know there could be other creatures down here, and nasty ones at that.' Lyndi Lou began to cry again.

'Look, what you've gone and done,' fumed Henratty.

'Don't blame me, Henratty – I'm not the one that mentioned monsters and nasty stuff,' refuted Jack.

'Lyndi Lou, I'm sorry I didn't mean to scare you; I was just trying to make Jack realise how serious our predicament was, because if we don't get out of here, we could be in serious danger and this torch is our only hope. Now let's press on,' commanded Henratty.

'Okay, sis, you're right. I'll try not to get too upset and instead focus on being positive about getting out of here,' Lyndi Lou said reassuringly.

'Have you got that, Jack ... FOCUS!' Henratty said sternly.

'Yeah, yeah, but I tell you there's treasure to be found here, I know it,' Jack responded defiantly.

'Let's go left here and tread carefully,' instructed Henratty.

CHAPTER THREE

Where's Enoch

Nora had listened with intent to their conversation:

So they think they're on a treasure hunt, well I think I better let Cooper know that they could possibly know about the hidden diamonds. How could they know about that I wonder? It is only Cooper and I that know about the diamonds and their whereabouts. It looks like they may not be so innocent after all. We'll definitely have to interrogate them to ensure they suspect nothing and dispel any idea of this mine being a treasure trove.

We have kept this place safe for thirty years and safe it must remain. These diamonds can only bring evil upon the land and if those evil birds of prey, the Larkans, in Skylark, get hold of them, it spells the end of this world as we know it. For the moment, there was no danger of that happening, as Nora with Cooper's help would ensure that these creatures never got out of this tunnel to tell the tale but for now, she would just observe to see what unfolds and what they truly know!

With those thoughts of Skylark buried once more, Nora began to wonder what was taking Enoch so long, it's never taken him this long to deliver a message before and Cooper and the others should have arrived by now.

* * *

29

Meanwhile, Enoch had finally realised something was wrong, as it dawned on him that it usually took him fifteen minutes at the most to walk back to base but he felt like he had been walking for all eternity. He was sure that at least thirty minutes had passed and he had not caught sight of base. In fact, as he looked more closely at the intricacies of the tunnel, he realised that this tunnel was completely different to the usual tunnel that had taken him back to base. For starters, the lights were much higher up the walls than the usual tunnel and it was a lot more dusty.

'Oh, no I must have taken the wrong turning; I told Nora that we should have marked the tunnels more clearly to define them, as she knows how easily I get confused. She is going to kill me or even worse she is going to insist that I eat Poppy to show that I am truly a mole, instead of the forgetful useless mole I know she thinks I am ...'

Poor Enoch wanted to shout "help" from the rooftops but that would only make things worse. Also he did not want to be the one that was to blame for alerting the visitors to the fact that they were no longer the only inhabitants in the mine.

Enoch continued to babble and revisit what he was going to do as he continued along the tunnel. Unbeknown to him the intruders were heading straight towards him.

'Shush,' Henratty commanded.

'What's wrong?

'I thought I heard something, or more like someone talking.'

'You must be hallucinating, surely there can't be anyone else down here,' remarked Jack.

'OH, NO – WHAT AM I GOING TO DO – I'M IN BIG TROUBLE!' uttered the voice – it was Enoch!

'Did you all hear that?' Everyone's eyes were wide open as they shook their heads in approval.

'Now be quiet,' Henratty whispered and then she switched the torch off. All of the meerkats were now pressed against the side of the wall, as Enoch scurried around the corner towards them, still jabbering to himself.

'Oh, no, I'm in so much trouble. Nora is going to string me up when she finds out that I have not gone back to base to warn the others.'

If only he had turned to his right, he would have seen four pairs of eyes staring back at him from the darkest corner of the tunnel, but what he would not have realised was how petrified they were of him. Enoch continued along the path, he was so disorientated by now and decided to stop where he was and take stock and try to retrace his steps. He turned around and started to make his way back down the tunnel as the four meerkats shot back into the darkest crevice again, holding their breaths once more.

'*What was that?*' Enoch murmured. He could have sworn that he heard a shuffling sound, but was not sure but then thought perhaps it was an echo of his own movements as he scuttled along the tunnel trying to retrace his steps. He turned right into the tunnel which he was sure would lead him back to Nora. He knew it was at least half an hour back to her and he could then find base from there having got his bearings back.

'What on earth was that?' asked Oscar.

'Whatever it was, it was bigger than us, but he sure did sound lost, and who was he talking about. He mentioned the name, *Nora,* so now we know there are at least two other animals down here besides us, which means we are not alone after all,' noted Henratty.

'I'm scared,' murmured Lyndi Lou.

'We're all scared … I think that creature is our safest bet of getting out of here – we have to follow him,' suggested Henratty.

'But he could be dangerous,' argued Oscar.

'Unfortunately, we don't have a choice, he is our only hope and we must follow him. I think he is a safe distance away now, so let's get a move on.' Henratty gave the torch to Jack which he switched back on, but he had to give it a good shake as the battery was dying. As it shone up towards the ceiling of the tunnel, he thought he saw something shimmering, but he had just shone the torch in his eyes so assumed he had been blinded by this which had distorted his vision. For a fleeting moment, he thought of the diamonds until his name was called:

'Come on, Jack, I think you should go first, seeing as you have the torch and the fact that we know you have the best hearing.'

'Sure thing, but let me just get my catapult out.'

'Er – what for?'

'What do you think for – these creatures could be dangerous and I need to be ready to fight back.'

'And a catapult is going to save us?' retaliated Henratty.

'Well, have you got any better ideas?'

'Yes, shut up and let's get a move on. The best thing we can do is try to remain out of sight and not get caught. By the way give me the other catapult, I'll give it to Oscar just in case! Now let's turn right here,' ordered Henratty.

'Are you sure, why not left?' demanded Jack.

'I definitely know he turned right, as I heard the creature say so, he constantly says everything out loud and he definitely said "right". So, be quiet and start listening, as we need to keep up with this creature so he can show us the way out, at least.' Everyone was on tiptoe as they moved along the tunnel, again in single file, desperately trying to keep out of Enoch's sight.

* * *

By now Nora could tell that something was wrong, everything was just too quiet, she could no longer hear the meerkats talking and where was Enoch?

'The bumbling buffoon, I gave him one simple task to complete and he could not even do that, the others should have been here at least twenty minutes ago!' she whinged.

Nora decided that she was going to have to fly back to base. She had not flown in ages and her joints were a little stiff, but she hoped and prayed that her wings would still enable her to fly. She had not used them in years, there was no real need to. She slowly opened her wings as her bones creaked. It's all or nothing, and with one big flap, she flew off. She could feel the strain as she gathered more strength to fully spread her wings and at last she was truly flying. She started to wobble, as she was losing momentum and speed. She was descending and could no longer soar as high but she was nearly there as she made a bumpy landing and slid on the ground as she flew in. She folded her wings. Her hair was a little mangled from the flight but she would fix it later.

As she entered camp, Cooper, Alfonso, Poppy and Escargot were all seated at the meeting table, anxiously awaiting her return.

'Has anybody seen Enoch?' screamed Nora.

'No, we thought he was with you. Is everything all right, Nora?' asked Cooper.

'Do I look all right? Nancy, can you please fix my hair, it's an absolute mess? I have just flown in and my wings are so rusty, I don't even know how I landed in one piece, luckily the only damage was to my hair!' Nancy was a whiz when it came to hair. She was a hedgehog and was very domesticated, indeed, and was responsible for keeping the dormitories spick and span; she just loved cleaning, cooking, etc and was a dab hand at these chores. She never complained at all. She ended up in the mine when she and her brother, Jasper, were captured by a family who wanted a pair of hedgehogs, but they managed to escape when the father got blind drunk and he forgot to lock their cage. They managed to trek from town to town, never staying in one place for too long until just by luck, and their love for strawberries, they stumbled upon Meerville Strawberry Fields. Also, they actually felt at home in Meerville, for some reason it was less threatening, but they could never work out why!

'I'm aching all over, I haven't flown in years and did not expect to ever fly again. Just wait until I get my hands on Enoch …'

'But what exactly has happened, Nora?' asked Cooper.

'Well, our little intruders have arrived, there are four of them, they sound pretty harmless but I think they are heading our way and that's why I sent Enoch back more than an hour ago to ask him to bring some of you back – particularly you, Cooper, Alfonso and Jasper for back up.'

'He must have taken the wrong turning,' said Poppy. 'You know how forgetful he is, or even worse could the beasts have perhaps captured him? If that's the case he has probably blurted out everything including our plot to capture them.'

'I think you could be right, especially on the first point, but I doubt if he has even remembered the plot and is probably still trying to show them a way to get back to base with great difficulty,' advised Cooper.

'Anyway, Cooper and I are going to use the one and only tramline that is still working to try and cut them off at the other side of the mineshaft. The last sound I received with my echolocation indicated that the little creatures were on that side of the shaft, so I am sure we can go round and cut them off.'

'But, Nora, why me, you know I can barely walk – can't Alfonso go?'

'I would prefer it if you came, Cooper, and besides you don't have to walk as we are taking the tram. Also you need the exercise, you can't stay cooped up in this hole all the time, that's probably why you're so hunched and cranky these days.'

'There's no need to get personal.'

Escargot had come out of his shell and was sniggering. As much as he tried to sleep, the increased volume of voices were resounding in his shell and getting louder and louder in decibels so he could not sleep even if he wanted to. Also the conversation became interesting, especially as Cooper was being chastised by Nora and had been given his marching orders, something Cooper was not used to, and something that Escargot revelled in. *That will teach the miserable coot*, he thought.

Under duress, Cooper gave in and off they went.

'Just before we depart, Alfonso, I want you to take charge, be vigilant and look out for our intruders. I'm sure once they set their eyes on you, they'll be wishing they were somewhere else.'

'Will do, Nora ... how exciting! Right folks you heard Nora, I'm in charge and therefore you all must do as I say.' Escargot was already back asleep in his shell, whilst Nancy and Jasper were dusting and buffing the already shiny ornaments and Poppy was gazing at herself in the cracked mirror preparing for the visitors.

'Did you hear what I said? I'm in charge so you must do as I say,' repeated Alfonso.

'But you have not asked us to do anything!' quipped Poppy, as she began to gurgle ...

'Well, when I do, I expect you all to comply,' commanded Alfonso.

'Naturally,' Jasper responded sarcastically.

* * *

Back in the tunnel, Enoch was still repeating himself and going on about how Nora was going to skin him alive when she found out he had not delivered the message.

The meerkats were only a few yards behind him now.

'What's wrong with him, he constantly talks to himself and has repeated the same sentence at least fifteen times. He's seriously barmy.'

'*Shhhh*! Jack.'

Suddenly, Enoch stopped talking aloud in mid sentence as he was convinced that he had just heard something, and it or they were close. His heart was beating faster and increasing in rate with every second. He felt scared, *Could it be the intruders,* he wondered. Part of him hoped so but the other half hoped not, as he was outnumbered; he knew there were four of them but only one of him. *Oh, no what was he going to do – okay, stay calm*, he thought. Suddenly he heard a noise again.

'Who's there, you're surrounded,' pretended Enoch, hoping his enemies would think he was not all by himself in the tunnel. But there was not a sound from anyone. Enoch now stood motionless and gripped with fear, the dark still air made him even more scared.

Suddenly he heard this growling bearlike sound which made Enoch instantly turn and shoot off down the tunnel, as he almost knocked himself out turning the corner, having sustained a gash on his head from a sharp piece of stone sticking out of the wall as he exited one tunnel into another.

'OH ... NO ... HELP ... HELP ... NORA,' he bellowed at the top of his voice. 'I need your help.'

When Enoch was out of sight, everyone breathed a sigh of relief as Jack started to cackle.

'What did you do that for?' said Henratty.

'Someone had to do something, he knew we were there and I could tell he was wetting himself with fear so I thought I'd scare him using Papa Brian's foghorn. Everyone's scared of bears and you all know I'm pretty good at impersonating other animal sounds. So how about thanking me for saving your lives?'

'Er – thanks, Jack, but now you have alerted him to our presence and he is on his way to let the other inhabitants know where we are.'

'They have to find us first, so I suggest we get off this tunnel and take the other tunnel going the other way until we can strategise and work out our co-ordinates,' Jack instructed in battle mode.

'We're not at war, so be serious, Jack. However, your idea seems a good one, so let's turn back. I think I noticed another tunnel on the left so we'll take that one and see where that leads us to. Let's not forget that we need to remain quiet at all times, as we are by no means safe,' reminded Henratty.

CHAPTER FOUR

Diamonds And Bears

Meanwhile Nora and Cooper were in the tram heading in the direction of Enoch.

'So, Nora, what was so important that you had to drag an old stick like me out of my comfort zone, when we have Jasper and Alfonso who are more able-bodied to capture these creatures.

'Oh, stop grumbling, you need to get out more, Coop!'

'Now look who's being ironic, it's not as if you go anywhere yourself and as you said you haven't even flown properly in years!'

'Cooper, don't be like that – you know what I mean: you need to exercise more, that's why you're so moody and hunched, it's not good. Anyway, I needed to speak to you away from prying eyes, it's important.' *What could possibly be so important,* he wondered.

'They know about the diamonds.' For the first time Cooper raised his head and was no longer hunched over. He was now staring at Nora taking in what she had just said.

'What do you mean, they know about the diamonds? How...When...Who...?

'Don't even try to think, at this stage I don't know how they know, in fact, I'm not a hundred percent convinced they know.'

'I'm confused, Nora, either they do or don't know about the diamonds, so which is it?'

'BOTH, one of the creatures mentioned the word diamonds but I am not sure in what context, as the one that said it, seemed to be speculating whether there could be diamonds and was not absolutely certain, if that makes sense. He sounded a little bit of a dreamer, but once we have captured the little mites, all will be revealed!'

* * *

Ten minutes later further along the track, Nora thought she had heard something a little way away but her echolocation was definitely picking something up, this she was certain of.

'Can you be quiet for a second, Cooper, I think I heard something.'

'Help … help … Nora … help … Alfonso … Cooper… Jasper… help…'

Enoch's voice was becoming more audible, Nora could hear more clearly now, she thought it sounded like Enoch. *What on earth was he doing on this side of the mine?* 'The bumbling idiot,' she called him once more.

'What is it?' Cooper asked.

'More like, who is it! It's that stupid mole, Enoch, and he sounds distressed, I think he's calling for help but he's coming our way so we'll pick him up. He can't be in that much danger as he's still talking and running, sounds like something has scared the living daylights out of him though, we'll soon find out what,' said Nora.

Enoch had stopped bawling for the moment as he could hear the wheels of the old tram in the distance. He was hoping and praying that it was Nora, Alfonso or Jasper.

'Hello! Hello!' he shouted, waving his arms in the air. 'Nora, is that you?'

'Yes, Enoch,' she snapped. 'Stay where you are, we're almost there, I don't want to run you over with the tram,' although she was tempted to. *The waste of space,* she thought to herself. She grabbed the handle controlling the tram as she started to slow it down, until finally it came to a crunching halt as the wheels screeched on the rusty tracks – they could certainly do with some oiling, *A lovely job for Enoch after his blunders today!* decided Nora.

'Oh, Nora, I'm so glad you are here, I lost my way back to camp, I must have gone down the wrong tunnel and did not realise for ages. I decided to retrace my steps but then I heard something in the tunnel. I proceeded to ask who was there, when suddenly I heard them. I know what these creatures are,' declared Enoch and then he took a long pause.

'Well, don't keep us guessing,' groaned Cooper. 'Tell us then. What are they?'

'Bears!' he said in a shaky voice.

'Bears ... bears ...' repeated Nora.

'Yes, bears.' Nora now had Enoch by the scruff of his neck and was pulling on his tie, as it tightened around his neck.

'You're choking me, Batty,' he wheezed, as she let go of her grip.

'Don't be so ridiculous, you buffoon, they cannot be bears; these creatures are small, not large.'

'Then they must be baby bears!' retorted Enoch.

'Now you're really being ridiculous.'

'I'm telling you they're bears, one of them growled at me. I've never been so scared in my life; I scooted out of that tunnel before you could say "bear" and I nearly knocked myself out in the process because I was that scared.' Something had definitely frightened Enoch, that was evident, but Nora was adamant they were not bears, far too small and gentle for bears.

'Oh, get in, Enoch! We're going back to camp to work things out. Now, be quiet – you're just not making sense. I want you to think carefully about what happened in that tunnel as we have to let the others know our next course of action, so we are relying on you for accurate information and "no" storytelling.'

For the moment all Enoch could think about was that growling bear and he was not going back in any tunnels. *He did not sign up for this,* he thought to himself, *to be eaten alive by bears ...*

✳ ✳ ✳

The meerkats were now becoming restless and frustrated; they all felt like they were going around in circles.

'Let's take a short break and have some of the strawberries that we collected but we must ration these to make them last, after all we have no way of knowing how long we are going to be down here,' as Henratty gave everyone an equal portion of strawberries. Jack looked down grumpily at the amount of strawberries he had been given. Henratty saw his reaction but she did not give him a chance to speak.

'Oh, please don't start. If you had used your brain in the first place we would probably have been rescued by now.'

'I see, like that is it, Henratty. Well, if you had not ignored that trespassing sign in the first place we would not even be down here, so there would be no need to blame me for a foiled rescue.'

'Will you two stop arguing for once,' pleaded Oscar. 'We have more important things to talk about. I say that we have no choice but to go back to the tunnel where we heard that inhabitant. He obviously knew the way out and had decided to turn back after Jack had scared him and I think he knew where he was going, having realised where he had gone wrong, if that makes sense. I don't think we have a choice anymore.'

'Yes, I agree with Oscar,' said Lyndi Lou, 'I just want to get out of here. He did sound pretty harmless – I think he was more frightened of us than we were of him, so how scary could the others be?'

'That's debatable but all right, I think we need to take a vote: I say we should carry on along this tunnel rather than walking into enemy hands. All those in favour of staying on this path, stick their hand up.' Only one hand was up in the air and that was Henratty's. She rolled her eyes in dismay but knew she had to go with their decision, albeit reluctantly.

'I guess the decision is unanimous then, we go back to the other tunnel and try to work out from there where the creature was heading. I reckon if Jack's torch holds out, we should be able to see footprints left by the creature and follow those. So eat up and let's get going,' suggested Henratty.

Indeed, they found the tunnel where Enoch had gone. They could also see a speck of blood on the ground where he had perhaps injured himself when he panicked. They followed his footprints which were clearly visible. He was definitely a fairly big animal but not as big as they had initially imagined.

It felt like they had walked for miles when suddenly they saw a flicker of light in the distance. *This looks promising, but could it be a trap, they hoped not but it was a journey they would have to take and suffer the consequences,* they all thought.

Jack led the party towards the lights and as they turned the corner he realised that this tunnel had newer tracks on it. *What a lucky find,* so he thought.

'Look guys,' as he aimed the torch down on the tracks. These are working tracks – I bet if we follow these they will lead us to the shaft exit. The mine obviously had working trams at some point to take all the diamonds over ground.

'For the last time, they weren't mining for diamonds,' reiterated Henratty.

'It's a matter of opinion, they're not exactly going to broadcast to the whole of Meerville the fact that there were diamonds down here, so I'm not convinced you're right, we'll see,' retorted Jack. Henratty then shook her head in disbelief at Jack's notion and decided it was best she ignored anymore suggestions of diamonds from Jack and let him play out his fantasy by himself.

The discovery of the tracks had certainly restored the meerkats' confidence somewhat, but little did they realise that these tracks would only lead them straight to the inhabitants' base, exactly where they didn't want to be.

Jack thought it was a good time for everybody to have a sip of water as he passed around his water tank and on they marched.

The lights only seem to illuminate part of the way and as they got further up the tunnel they were in pitch darkness again and at this point he got his torch out. *Indeed, Nora's plan was working, she had suggested that they turn the lights out along the tunnel in order to restrict their visitors' visibility as far as possible so they could easily ambush them, as well as make it much harder for them to find a way out, not that there really was a way out, or was there?*

* * *

Nora, Cooper and a distraught Enoch had arrived back at base.

'Look they've found Enoch,' spouted Poppy. 'Oh, Enoch, so glad you are safe. What have you done to your face?'

'Oh, nothing, I gashed it on a sharp stone on the corner of the exit of the tunnel when I was running for my life.'

'What actually happened?' Enoch explained how he had lost his way and ended up in the tunnel system on the other side of the mineshaft and as he started to retrace his steps he heard a noise and the next thing he knew he was being chased by a bear.

'A bear,' they all said. 'How on earth did a bear get down here?'

'Now folks, don't listen to Enoch, it was no bear. These creatures are very small, probably not much bigger than Jasper,' uttered Nora.

'Well, all I can say is that I heard a bear growl at me and I know what noise a bear makes, so believe me or don't believe me, I don't care anymore ...'

'Enoch, you poor thing!' said Jasper. 'How are we ever going to fight off four bears?'

'We're not,' said Cooper. 'Did you not hear Nora say they were not bears?'

'But Enoch heard them with his own ears,' reminded Jasper.

'But did you actually see the creatures?' Cooper enquired.

'Not exactly ...' replied Enoch.

'Well, Nora heard the creatures talking earlier and she has the best hearing out of all of us, so I believe her when she said they were not bears,' stressed Cooper.

Surprisingly, Nora had remained quiet throughout their conversation as she was thinking carefully about the next course of action. Nancy had made everyone a cup of strawberry tea as they all sat around the table. They sipped on the delicious tea, apart from Escargot who was fast asleep as per usual. Nancy tapped on his shell to wake him up as she left a saucer of tea for him and out popped his head.

'Have I missed anything? Um, strawberry tea – thank you, Nancy,' as he inhaled the scent of the sickly sweet strawberries and siphoned some of the tea.

'I suspect the little creatures are heading this way, as they obviously know they were not the only ones down here in this mine and were looking for a way out. They would have thought Enoch could lead them to the actual way out, which is why I suspect they were following him as they heard him talking to himself in the tunnel – you were talking to yourself again, I take it, Enoch?' He looked a little embarrassed but confessed: 'Yes I'm sorry, it's the only way I remember things!'

'Right I suggest that Alfonso, Enoch and Jasper come with me and bring that net with you. I should be able to hear the creatures when they are fairly close and as they come out of the tram tunnel into the camp tunnel, we will capture them with this net. I will act as bait and hang above the little creatures to distract them and then you can throw the net,' suggested Nora.

'What a brilliant idea,' remarked Cooper.

'We don't have much time left, so come with me and the rest of you, please be vigilant, as they could be smarter than we think and come from the other side of the tunnel but that would mean they won't get here until much later, judging by where Enoch said he had heard them. So, are we ready?' asked Nora.

'Yes, Nora,' and off they went.

CHAPTER FIVE

Our Meerkats Are Missing

Back at the Mortimers' house, Mama Mortimer was starting to get a little worried, as she looked at the clock. It was gone five and still no sign of Henratty and Lyndi Lou. She just had this sick feeling that something was wrong. She decided to wait a little longer as Papa Mortimer would be home shortly and then they could consider what they should do.

She was just about to put the kettle on, when the door bell rang. She jumped with excitement as she thought it must be her little ones who had forgotten their keys. Well, who else would be ringing the door bell? She quickly turned the tap off and set the kettle to boil as she rushed to the front door.

'Henratty, what have you done with your keys?' she demanded but to her surprise it was neither Henratty nor Lyndi Lou at the door, but Mama Katie.

'Have you heard from Henratty or Lyndi Lou by any chance?' said Mama Katie anxiously.

'No, I would have asked you the same question. All I know is that they were going strawberry picking with your Jack and Oscar. They're not usually this late but

I know Henratty would never do anything silly and just assumed they had gone back to yours.'

'I'm afraid not,' as Mama Katie entered the Mortimers' house.

'Papa Mortimer is going to be home in a minute, so when he arrives, we'll decide what to do then. I've just put the kettle on – would you like a cup of tea?' stated Mama Mortimer.

'Thank you that would be nice. I have left a message with the receptionist for Papa Brian to call me straightaway as he was off site, but she could not get hold of him immediately and insisted she would keep trying. He may call here as I said it was an emergency and explained my concern,' confided Mama Katie.

Suddenly, the telephone rang, as they looked at each other trying not to think the worse, but thinking the worse. It was Papa Brian, as Mama Mortimer passed the telephone to Mama Katie. She began to explain what had happened. Papa Brian advised that Papa Mortimer would be there soon and they were to meet him at the strawberry fields in an hour. Although worried he felt sure that their meerkats had probably just decided to stay out late and were probably on their way home having lost track of time.

* * *

Within an hour both parents were now outside the gates of Meerville Strawberry Fields. It was six o'clock! Noticeably, the gates were locked and there was no sign of the attendant.

'Well, they can't be here', said Papa Brian. 'There's no way that the attendant would have locked them in.

However, I think we should give him a call on the emergency number when we get home to see if he can remember seeing them leave.' He took out his pen and paper and jotted down the telephone number and off they headed back home. As the Brians were the nearest they decided to go to their house first of all, but there was still no sign of their little meerkats.

'I bet they're at our house,' insisted Papa Mortimer as they sped off down the road towards the Mortimers.

As Papa Mortimer, opened the door, he called out for Henratty, Lyndi Lou, Oscar and Jack, but there was complete silence. This time Papa Brian really was worried as he frowned at Mama Katie and then asked Papa Mortimer if he could use the telephone.

'Is that you, Gladstone? It's Papa Brian.'

'Why hello and what can I do for you?'

'Did you happen to see my Jack and Oscar with their friends, Henratty and Lyndi Lou, at the strawberry fields today? You know Jack, he's slightly larger than the other meerkats and possibly would have been wearing his army jacket, also you can't miss Henratty, as she would have been wearing a red beret and red cape.

'Er – now you mention it, I do recall vaguely seeing someone of her description but I have to say we had quite a lot of visitors today and I can't remember everyone.'

'If you could please try to remember, this is very important. Did you see them leave?'

'I'm not sure, as I don't man the gate all the time, and earlier today, a group of meerkats got into a scuffle so I was distracted for a little while. The only thing I can be sure of is that I always announce when it's time to lock up and I also check the area for any visitors who may have got carried away with picking strawberries and ignored my last reminder and I can tell you that *no one* was left in those fields before I locked up! I do recall the attendant that was on duty yesterday reminding me to ensure that I double checked the fields as he almost locked in some meerkats and he was a little alarmed as he did not see them when inspecting the fields, but they apologised and said they would take extra care next time.'

'Okay, thanks very much but if you do hear anything could you let us know as it is very unusual for Jack and his friends to be out so late without telling us they were going to be back later than usual.'

'Will do and I will try to speak to the attendant to see if he noticed anything suspicious the day before, but usually we record anything like that and as I've just mentioned it was only those two meerkats!'

As Papa Brian came off the telephone he looked at Mama Katie and the Mortimers and shook his head to indicate that it was not good news.

'I am going to call the sheriff now to advise that our meerkats are missing. I think Papa Mortimer and I should then head into town to see if they have ended up there. We'll need a couple of pictures,' said Papa Brian, as Mama Katie fetched a few photos she had kept in her handbag luckily from Oscar's birthday party, which included Henratty and Lyndi Lou too.

CHAPTER SIX

The Ambush

Whilst Nora, Jasper, Alfonso and Enoch were on their way back to the tram heading towards their visitors, the meerkats were still following the tram tracks and heading right for the base camp as Nora had predicted.

'How much further do you think we have to go?' Oscar requested.

'Don't ask such stupid questions,' replied Jack. How am I supposed to know? Do I look like I've ever been in this tunnel before?'

'It's just that Lyndi Lou and I are tired – can't we rest for five minutes?'

'All right, just five minutes and then we are on our way, I don't think I can stand another minute down here,' moaned Henratty. As they huddled in the corner, Jack passed around his water tank once again and they ate a handful more strawberries.

'I don't think I can eat another strawberry,' protested Lyndi Lou, 'I'm sick of the sight of them.' How ironic, as earlier she was only saying how much she loved strawberries!

'Well, that's all we have so you better get used to it,' Henratty asserted firmly, as Jack pulled out a small brown bag from his pocket. He then proudly said, 'Would anyone like a bonbon?'

'Yes please,' beamed Lyndi Lou and Oscar.

'There you go, take a few, as I have some more in the other pocket.' This little gesture by Jack could not have come at a better moment, as it acted as a temporary distraction from the grave situation the meerkats were all in; their frustration was certainly starting to show outwardly. It was times like this that Jack not only showed his remarkable ability to defuse any situation but that he deeply cared despite him being thick-skinned most of the time, an action that had not gone unnoticed by Henratty, as she smiled to herself.

* * *

Nora had finally reached a good place in the tunnel where she felt visibility would be extremely limited and it was on a bend. She brought the tram to a halt.

'Why are we stopping here, whined Enoch?'

'Don't you ever listen to anything I say? Must I repeat myself? This is where you three are going to ambush our little visitors whilst I distract them from above. I will wait until they get within reaching distance to me, and then alert them to my presence so that they start running away from me in the direction of the net that you will be holding on either side of the tunnel and then you can pin them down with it. Is that clear?' asked Nora.

'Absolutely,' replied Enoch. 'Alert, scare, then ambush, I've got it in three.'

'Don't you mean *one*, Enoch?' He was confused as he just gazed at Nora, who said, 'Don't even answer that!

Now please get ready ... I'm going to wait a bit further up the tunnel. I will be hanging above them so they won't see me, and you only have to listen for their screams to know that they are coming.'

'Okay, Nora, we've got you loud and clear,' affirmed Alfonso.

'Main lights out,' ordered Nora as she disappeared around the corner into the pitch black tunnel.'

'I can't wait to bite the little creatures, especially if they start to resist our ambush,' Alfonso hissed.

'I just hope for our sake they're not bears as Nora seemed to think. Oh, the thought of being clawed by a bear is just unthinkable,' as Enoch took a big gulp and held his tummy feeling sick just from the very thought.

'Enoch, shut up and focus – be quiet,' snapped Jasper. 'We have work to do!'

*   *   *

Nora was in position above the tunnel some thirty yards away from the trap that Enoch, Alfonso and Jasper were laying. She was suspended and just wanted to go back to her meditation, but had no choice, as she knew these creatures must be found soon and interrogated about the diamonds. Her echolocation had picked them up again; they were on the move and steadily coming her way. Another ten minutes and they would be there, as she waited patiently and quietly, fully camouflaged in the darkness. Naturally, it helped being a bat!

Jack started to bang the torch as it shimmered on and then went off intermittently, each time he shook the torch even harder than the last time.

'What's wrong?' asked Henratty

'The battery has died,' said Jack glumly, as complete darkness fell upon them once more.

'We're just going to have to somehow follow the tracks and make use of our outstretched arms to feel our way through the tunnel and just hope this is enough to ensure we don't bump into anything serious,' recommended Henratty.

Further up the tunnel, Nora had just heard Jack shaking the torch.

At last, the little visitors had arrived, and Nora was more than ready for them. She just hoped both Alfonso and Jasper in particular, had understood her instructions to capture these creatures. Nora had told them to leave one small light on at the corner of the tunnel to steer the creatures the right way and hoped they had remembered!

'Here they are,' Nora murmured to herself.

They were only ten yards away from Nora, and Lyndi Lou was the first to notice the flickering light, but it was very dim and a little way in the distance.

'Look!' she whispered, 'I think there's some light further up – can you see it?'

'Yes we can,' they all replied quietly. Jack decided that he would test the torch once more as he took it out of his pocket. They were now standing underneath Nora, as the torch came back on. *Hooray*, they thought. Jack began to aim the torch down the tunnel when suddenly he heard a weird sound, like a flapping motion.

'What was that?'

'WHAT WAS WHAT?' said Henratty.

'I could swear I heard something moving. It sounded like wings!' Jack responded.

Very astute, he could almost be a bat, thought Nora, but she knew he was not.

Nora flapped her wings once more, as the meerkats gasped. They were all frozen solid, as if time had stopped, the tunnel felt ice cold but that's because they were gripped with fear. Jack suddenly shone the torch in the direction he had heard the sound. Nora flapped her wings again but not so dramatically, she did it in a very slow but controlled motion. The meerkats jumped as this time there was no doubt that they had definitely heard something. The torch was shining brighter than ever, as the intense beam of light smacked Nora right between the eyes.

'My eyes, my eyes,' Nora shrieked. 'Can you turn that torch off at once?' But Jack was intrigued and wanted to know who was there. He had already calculated that if these inhabitants were going to harm them, they would have done so already, so he retaliated:

'Who's there – you don't scare us?'

'We have a brave one in our midst,' whispered Nora, as she then flapped her wings frantically, which made the torch fall out of Jack's hand, as it plunged to the ground.

'Now listen here, I warned you to turn that torch off. My eyes are very sensitive and I suffer from photophobia, and if you shine that torch once more that will be the last time you see anything for a long time,' Nora barked infuriatingly.

'Photo what?' but before Jack knew it, the other meerkats were screaming and running towards the dimly lit tunnel in the distance. As Jack swivelled round, his eyes were met by a pair of menacing red eyes, wildly peering at him.

'Er – yikes,' he whimpered as he ducked, grabbed his torch and began to run towards the glowing light. He had now caught up with the other meerkats, but as they turned the corner of the tunnel they were thrown backwards, almost as if they had been hit with some sort of elastic and fell to the ground – down came the net as they screamed even louder, Lyndi Lou's scream being the highest pitch they had ever heard.

Nora had descended and had now joined the other animals, as she said, 'Enoch, go and put the lights back on in the tunnel.'

'But can't I stay here, after all I was the one that led them to you?'

'ENOCH!' she hooted.

'Yes, yes, Nora, the lights … the lights … I'm going!'

'Now little ones, I think we've heard enough screams to last a lifetime; it's pointless screaming anymore, no one's going to hear you except us.' Indeed, the meerkats were silent. Visibility was still quite poor in the tunnel, especially under that net, but they could just about make out Nora who was now standing in front of them and looking really angry. They now realised she was a bat, but they still had no idea what her companions were who remained in the background.

Enoch had eagerly just returned. He did not want to miss his moment of glory having been the one that had enabled the meerkats to be captured, ultimately.

'Honestly, Enoch, they're not bears,' chortled Alfonso.

'I can see that now. Well, what are they?'

'You have got to be kidding … have you never seen meerkats before? Why do you think the fields are called Meerville Strawberry Fields? It's because we're in meerkat territory – I thought you knew that!'

'Obviously, I've forgotten, but I still maintain I heard a bear in that tunnel and I'm not changing my mind!' Enoch said adamantly.

'I demand that you let us out of here,' protested Henratty.

'At last they speak ...' said Alfonso.

'Now which one of you was shining that torch in my face? Ah, it was you,' as Nora pointed to Jack.

'And yes it was me ... so what and what's photophobia?'

'I see you're not as bright as I thought, because if you knew what photophobia was you would have stopped shining that torch in my eyes,' as Jasper, Enoch and Alfonso started laughing.

'Shut up, you three!' barked Nora, as she began to release the meerkats from the net.

'Now get up and come with me. I suggest you don't run as there's no way out of here anyway and you would just be wasting your time,' instructed Nora to the meerkats. At which point, all the meerkats just looked at each other horrified at the possibility of never getting out of this awful place. They dusted themselves off once more and followed her back to the tram.

'Get in and be quiet, especially you *torch boy*!'

'By the way, I do have a name you know – you can call me Jack!'

'INSOLENT JACK! Now, shut up, before I shut you up!' retorted Nora, as Henratty nudged Jack and gave him that look which he knew meant to zip it or else!

There was one thing and one thing only that was going through their minds as Nora started up the tram and headed back towards camp. *Would they ever get out of this dark place alive?* Jack was already scheming as he glanced over at Henratty who was weaving a plan too, as she gazed at him.

They travelled in silence along the dimly lit tunnel. Fifteen minutes had now gone by. The tram then made a right turn as it stopped next to some old wooden doors, which suddenly sprung open.

'Now get out everybody and follow me,' commanded Nora.

At last there was proper lighting as the meerkats could now see who had, indeed, accompanied them in the tram. They could clearly see Enoch the mole and Jasper the hedgehog but were mortified to see Alfonso the rattlesnake as he began to hiss as if he wanted to attack them. *How could all these creatures live in one place and not have killed each other yet! It was truly amazing,* noted Henratty.

'Alfonso, will you please stop hissing ... now is not the time,' demanded Nora, as he recoiled back down in his seat and slithered out of the tram, followed by Jasper then Enoch who was muttering to himself, as usual.

Despite the imminent danger, there was no way Jack could keep quiet and just had to say something: 'I demand you show us the way out of here. We mean you no harm and it was a pure accident that we ended up down here.'

'*A pure accident?*' Nora taunted. 'Surely you can all read ... did you not see the sign about trespassing and what happens to trespassers: they are prosecuted and I am your prosecutor!' Lyndi Lou started to weep.

'Oh, look what you've done to my sister, you evil thing,' barked Henratty forgetting where she was for a second. 'Look I'm sorry, that came out all wrong; we just want to get out of here, so please let us go.'

'Maybe later but as I said there is no way out of this mine so you can forget that idea,' replied Nora. 'For now, you are all staying here.'

'Er – look here bat, we're not scared of you and be warned that the rest of Meerville Town have been alerted, it is only a matter of time before they come down here,' refuted Jack.

Nora was inches away from Jack's face as she glared at him.

'And how so, when I know you did not call for help before entering the mineshaft – a very foolish move, Jack, wouldn't you say?' as she poked him in the head as if to say, *What were you thinking?*

'Will you, please, all get out of the tram and follow me,' Nora reiterated and reluctantly they descended. Nora's intimidation had worked … they were scared that was for sure but Jack was the most determined not to show it, although he was a little scared inside.

CHAPTER SEVEN

Meet The Neighbours

As they walked past the giant wooden doors, they noticed there was another hedgehog who had opened the door as she shook her head acknowledging their arrival. It was Nancy of course, Jasper's sister, who was wearing her apron as per usual; she was never seen without it. They entered what seemed a much wider tunnel with alcoves leading off from it on either side, like dormitories. There were six in total, three on each side, from what they could make out.

Nora led them to the third dormitory on the right. The plaque on the door said "Master Cooper" and as the door swung open, they were greeted by all the other inhabitants they had not seen yet. They noticed a fire place straight ahead at the back of the dormitory that was being stoked by a rather hunched over creature who immediately turned around upon hearing them enter. It was Cooper the rat who said, 'Ah, Nora! At last ... so these are our little bears?' as the other inhabitants all burst out laughing.

'Okay, guys, so I made a mistake, bears – meerkats, what's the difference?' Enoch cowered.

'What was that about?' whispered Oscar.

'I think they were having a joke at Enoch's expense as he told them we were bears after Jack growled at him with his foghorn.' *If only that were true, how different the scenario would be right now,* thought Henratty.

To the right, near the fireplace there was a large bed in a small alcove. More or less in the centre of the room was a large wooden table with seating for ten. Some of the seats were already occupied by Enoch, Jasper and Alfonso. They also noted directly in front of the two seats nearest to them was a snail (or rather the shell of a snail), as well as the cutest looking worm they had ever seen. These two species were much larger than the average size one would expect, but what they were was undeniable.

Nora decided to rest her poor weary legs and sat down at the head of the table with Nancy sat to the right of her next to Cooper.

'Now little ones,' said Nora referring to the meerkats, 'I'm going to ask you a couple of questions so I suggest that you pay particular attention and give me the right answers.'

'You've got to be joking, this feels like we are being interrogated but we've not done anything wrong!'

'Can you ever keep quiet boy or will I have to make you keep quiet,' as Nora turned and looked at Alfonso subliminally insinuating that Alfonso could perhaps wrap himself around Jack to keep him quiet. Alfonso began to hiss as he raised his head up off the table. His shadow illuminated the walls of the dormitory and even though it was well lit, it was still quite a dark place, but in comparison to those unlit tunnels it was indeed bright. Alfonso then began to weave in and out of the crockery on the table heading towards Jack. The meerkats were now huddled together and shaking a little, except for Jack, as Alfonso began to raise the back of his tail off the table, but once again he had forgotten he could not rattle, as he dropped his tail, turned and slithered back to his seat.

'Now do you understand about keeping quiet?' Jack had got the message as he nodded his head without making a sound, but he only obeyed because he knew somehow these inhabitants were their ticket out of here. Besides Alfonso was a snake and he could take him out any time but he would have to contend with the other inhabitants as he knew he was outnumbered.

'So let's begin: Why were you in the prohibited strawberry fields, when the sign clearly stated, "*Danger and no trespassing*"?'

'It was my idea, the strawberries looked much bigger and juicier there and I thought what harm would there be to pick a few – no one noticed the first time,' admitted Henratty.

'Yes, I heard you and one other marching around the field. You both had a lucky escape that day, but then you came back with your tubby friend and his little brother,' as she glared at Jack suspiciously.

'Yes, only because we needed more strawberries for Mama Katie, Jack and Oscar's mother, so she could make her special strawberry tart and I promised I would show them the special place where we found the extra delicious strawberries in return for Mama Katie's recipe – it's really good,' Henratty answered exuberantly.

'Um – I see! Was there any other reason for you all being in that field?' Nora further demanded.

'What other reason could we possibly have, we were only interested in the strawberries ... isn't that why ... how you all ended up in this tunnel or were you all looking for something else?' enquired Henratty.

Enoch was the first to speak: 'Well, I got completely lost and did not see the sign in the dark. As you've probably gathered my memory is not the greatest and I'm constantly forgetting things.'

'Yeah, we've noticed,' declared Jack.

'I was grabbed by some kind of bird of prey who lost its grip and dropped me in the field and on landing, I rolled down a hole in the strawberry fields and ended up in the mineshaft, be it a little wounded but Nora nursed me back to health. All I have is a tiny scar from the claw of that creature,' uttered Poppy.

'And Jasper and I were captured by a family looking for pet hedgehogs. Luckily we managed to escape when he fell asleep in his truck, after pulling over at the side of the strawberry fields, and again we tumbled down the mineshaft and what a blessing in disguise that was. This is our home and we would like to keep it that way,' pronounced Nancy.

The meerkats then turned to Alfonso naturally expecting him to explain how he had ended up in the mine, but he merely gave them a stone-faced stare. From Alfonso's frosty reception, the meerkats immediately knew that he would be the one to watch closely, as he had definitely made them feel much more uneasy than the other inhabitants.

At that point, Escargot popped out of his shell, still half asleep which made the meerkats jump back in astonishment.

'It's only Escargot the snail,' said Poppy sweetly.

'What's all the commotion now, I never seem to be able to sleep of late. And who do we have here?' as he turned his weary face towards the meerkats.

'These are the little creatures that I heard in the strawberry fields the other day. As I suspected, it was only a matter of time before they ended up down here and here they are,' announced Nora.

'*Bonjour mes petits amis,*' said Escargot.

'What's he saying?' asked Jack.

'He said, "*Hello my little friends*",' explained Lyndi Lou.

'Why can't he just speak normally – it'll be much easier?' insisted Jack.

'I love speaking my beautiful language, so you better get used to it, *petit garçon*!'

'And what's with the "boy" all the time?' asked Jack.

'So you are not as dumb as you look, I see you understand my beautiful language.'

'Not really, I just know *garçon* means boy!'

Escargot then began to whinge about how stupid Jack was but no one could really understand what he was saying.

'Oh, be quiet Escargot! Not everyone has to speak French like you; there is just no need for it here ... so stop your ranting and if you have something to say make it constructive instead of that babble,' remarked Cooper.

Feeling insulted, Escargot looked at Cooper with an evil glint in his eye. He then sighed as he went back into his shell resentfully.

Apart from his last comment, Cooper, like Nora, had remained quiet throughout the recent discussion, not without Henratty and Jack noticing their constant eye to eye contact. They smelt a "rat" and were not just referring to Cooper! There was a lot more to their interrogation than meets the eye, but for now they needed to focus on getting out of this mine.

'So, how long have you all been down here?' asked Henratty bravely.

'Did I say you could ask any questions – I have not finished yet? What do you know of this mine?' demanded Nora.

'Nothing,' retorted Henratty, as she continued: 'I vaguely remember papa giving us a history lesson on Meerville Town but he only mentioned something in relation to the mine being shut down some thirty years or so ago, and that was it. He never mentioned its location and no one had ever talked about it since.'

Again, Nora glanced at Cooper, who had now moved over to his rocking chair; he always found the seats at the table very uncomfortable and much preferred his rocking chair!

'I think that is enough questioning for today. Jasper and Alfonso will show you to your sleeping quarters and we will continue this discussion tomorrow. Now take them away, they can stay in the spare dormitory until we decide what to do with them. If you all want to stay alive I suggest you follow Jasper and Alfonso and we'll resume this meeting tomorrow,' informed Nora.

As the meerkats entered the small, dingy and barely lit room, there were two wooden beds with a small table separating them. The lighting in here was even worse than the main dormitory but they could just about see each other, thankfully because of the fairly wide gap under the doorway which allowed much needed light into the dormitory. How they yearned for the cool fresh air and sunlight they so often took for granted.

'What was that all about? Those creatures are freaky, especially Cooper and Nora? Why were they questioning us like that? It definitely felt like they thought we knew something more about this mine – what could it be I wonder?' questioned Henratty.

'I definitely agree with you,' said Jack. I can't put my finger on it, but Nora and Cooper are hiding something and I don't even think the other inhabitants realise, as most of them call this mine their home and seem to be quite content living here and to a degree, I can almost understand why after they explained their ordeals. I guess here they feel safe from predators. Even though in theory one would have expected them to turn on each other, they seem to have lost their killer instinct and live together (it would appear in harmony) to survive. Enoch being forgetful does not even realise most of the time that he is a mole and should have eaten Poppy a long time ago, but you can see they really get on. Again, Nancy and Jasper should have gone for Poppy and Escargot as well, but they seem very domesticated.'

'Perhaps they have enough of a food source so never need to turn on each other,' noted Lyndi Lou.

'I could kiss you,' gleamed Jack.

'Oh, Jack, please. No thank you!'

'I don't mean kiss you literally, Lyndi Lou, I'll leave that to Oscar ...'

'You promised, JACK!' howled Oscar.

'Oh, get over it, we all know you have a crush on Lyndi Lou and I bet she knows it too,' Jack said amusingly.

'Jack, let's just get back to what you were trying to say,' interrupted Henratty.

'I think Lyndi Lou hit the nail on the head. It's way too dark down here for anyone to survive and bearing in mind how healthy they all look, I would say they have a pretty well maintained diet, so where is their food source? I say above ground and if it's above ground then there's a way out of here and I intend on finding it,' Jack beamed smugly.

'Jack, I don't know how you do it, but what you've just said makes sense. I think everyone is so exhausted, so it's best we sleep on your notion and try to come up with a plan of action tomorrow. Like you said, if they wanted us dead, they would have done something by now,' concluded Henratty.

CHAPTER EIGHT

The Search

Back in Meerville Town, the Brians and Mortimers had just left the sheriff's office to report that their meerkats were missing following a visit to the strawberry fields. They had also paid a visit to the attendant but he could not shed any light on where they may have gone, as he was adamant there was no one left in those fields before he locked up.

The sheriff decided that it was really too dark to commence a search and would utilise the rest of the day to hand out posters and resume a serious search tomorrow, beginning with the strawberry fields.

They had all decided to head back to the Mortimers' house, being nearer to the fields, still hopeful that Henratty, Lyndi Lou together with Jack and Oscar had made their way home, but as Papa Mortimer opened the door they were met with total darkness and silence.

Mama Mortimer began to cry as he consoled her whilst Mama Katie went to put the kettle on. Mama Katie was a very strong individual indeed, she always remained positive and refused to get too upset until she knew the facts for definite, unlike Mama Mortimer who was more emotional and could not hide her feelings of distress so easily.

Mama Mortimer had now joined Mama Katie in the kitchen whilst Papa Brian and Papa Mortimer were in the sitting room discussing an action plan for tomorrow. They had decided that they would get up at the crack of dawn and head down towards the strawberry fields to meet the attendant who would let them in, extra early, so they could search the fields thoroughly and see if Jack had left any clues. They knew how adventurous he was and if in danger, the only thing on his mind would be plotting to escape and leaving clues so they could be rescued.

* * *

At the first sign of light the next morning, Papa Brian and Papa Mortimer met the sheriff and the rest of the force along with the attendant who let them into Meerville Strawberry Fields. Not a sound could be heard at all. Each group of meerkats were given a specific area to cover ensuring that the whole field would be searched thoroughly, but their search was in vain.

'What about over there?' stated Papa Brian, as he pointed to the prohibited area with the trespassing sign.

'I think it is highly unlikely they would venture there, especially after seeing that warning sign – Henratty was very sensible and would never endanger anyone's life,' assured Papa Mortimer.

'Nor Jack for that matter,' commented Papa Brian.

'That field is above the old mine that was shut down thirty years or so ago. I don't know if you remember it, as you two would have been little then, but the ground became very unstable from all the mining and I'm afraid my force would be lost if they went in there,' said the sheriff.

'We do understand,' affirmed Papa Brian. 'We're just going to take a closer peek to see if we can find anything that might indicate they could have gone into that field.'

'If you must, but please be careful and stay on this side of the fence,' warned the sheriff.

Both parents approached the field with exceptional caution, holding onto each other in fear of the unstable ground giving way but they were still on the safe side of the fields, so there was no danger really. They scanned the area several times, however, nothing looked disturbed or out of the ordinary.

'There's no way they would have gone into that field, look there's no strawberries to pick anyway. One look at this field and you would definitely not even bother contemplating going in there especially with a sign like that. I guess because of the mining, nothing good grows here anyway!' presumed Papa Mortimer. It never dawned on them that perhaps there were no strawberries because, firstly, Jack had eaten most of them and, secondly, they had picked all the strawberries as there were so few in this field to begin with.

'You're right, nothing but wasteland,' agreed Papa Brian.'

* * *

It was just after two o'clock in the afternoon and so far no one in Meerville Town had come forward with any information that could lead to the possible whereabouts of Henratty, Jack, Oscar and Lyndi Lou. They had been missing for one whole day and something like this had not happened in a very long time and was virtually unheard of in Meerville. Papa Brian gave Mama Katie a worried glance; she knew what he was thinking when he looked at her solemnly. *Was history about to repeat itself – they both believed in The Meerville Myth. Had Dustmist arisen once more to wreak havoc on the Mortimers and Brians, as it was their very meerkats that had broken the spell and brought the Mortimers' eldest daughter, Misha, back safely? All they knew was that Dustmist had disappeared, which they had hoped was for good, but no one really knew.*

Papa Mortimer had picked up on Papa Brian's and Mama Katie's thoughts as he uttered, 'I bet I know what you were both thinking?'

'Was it that obvious?' asked Papa Brian.

'Yes, I'm afraid so, to tell the truth I was thinking the same thing, it's Dustmist isn't it? You both think Dustmist has come back for revenge starting with our little ones?'

'At this stage, we can't rule him out, it's the only thing that would make sense. At least Misha was safe. I think it was a good idea that you sent her away to stay with friends, but for now I don't think we can say anything to the sheriff. He would just laugh at us and say, *'Don't be so ridiculous – it's only a myth!'* remarked Papa Brian.

'Yes, at least that's one thing we are all in agreement with,' affirmed Papa Mortimer as he and Papa Brian looked at their respective partners.

'I don't think there is much more we can do in Meerville Town now. Something tells me that we should go back to the strawberry fields and take another look without the sheriff. If it were left to me I would have already taken a closer peek at the field above the mine; there is something that has been niggling me. I can't put my finger on it but when we go back there it will come to me,' said Papa Brian.

'Do you two think that is really a good idea?' sniffled Mama Mortimer, as she just about held back her tears. 'You heard what the sheriff said, it really *wasn't safe*, and what if the ground gives way?'

'Honey, I think it's a risk we have to take. At least if we go missing, you will definitely know where we are and can get help if need be, but I promise it won't come to that,' reassured Papa Mortimer.

'You promise?' repeated Mama Mortimer as she hugged Papa Mortimer lovingly.

'A promise is a promise,' chirped Papa Mortimer, but deep down he knew their suggestion could have serious consequences.

'Papa Brian does know what he is doing,' reassured Mama Katie confidently, although she did not feel as confident inside but if there was a slim chance that their little meerkats had ignored the trespassing sign, which in all probability was possible, then they had no choice but to try and find them.

They decided that as it was quite late in the afternoon, by the time they got to the fields, it would be too dark and they needed the best light possible when treading on such dangerous grounds to minimise any serious accident. They would take Papa Mortimer's pick-up truck from which one of them would be attached to a rope which was tied to the back of the truck, so that if the ground caved in, they could be hoisted back up to safety. Papa Brian volunteered to go into the fields, as he had some climbing experience whilst Papa Mortimer would operate the truck hoist, if need be.

So for tonight, they would go home and rest. They had been on their feet for most of the day and there really was nothing more that they could do physically.

CHAPTER NINE

Call My Bluff

Jack was the first to stir, he started to wriggle his nose as the sweet aroma of strawberries wafted up his nostrils and the smell of warm bread followed soon after. It was just about visible in the dark room thankfully due to the gap in the doorway. He could see a tray brimming with bread, an open jar of strawberry jam and a saucer with some butter. They were left one very blunt knife and in another tray were four plates, four empty glasses and a jug filled with strawberry juice. He quietly got out of bed as he checked the time on his watch. He had just remembered that the face of his watch would illuminate when it was tapped on twice, again another brilliant purchase by Papa Brian. He could not believe the time, it was three thirty in the afternoon and surely they had not been sleeping that long but then yesterday was no ordinary day, after all they had spent most of the day in those tunnels trying to find a way out and that was quite exhausting in itself!

No longer perturbed by the passage of time, Jack now glanced at the tray of food.

'Wake up everybody, we have food and it sure does smell good,' Jack cried.

Henratty was the first to rise after hearing what she called Jack's annoying voice. She quickly jumped up, as he felt a tap on his shoulder just before he was about to tuck into the food.

'Not so fast, Jack, we need to divide the food fairly.'

'Oh, come on, don't be like that, as if I would scoff the whole lot without a second thought for my friends and not to mention my younger brother. Do you honestly think I would do such a thing?'

'Frankly, at this moment in time I'm not sure, we are all in a very vulnerable state and our ultimate goal is survival.' Jack thought there was no point arguing with Henratty as she could be right. He knew what he was like once he started eating and sometimes he just could not stop himself, not because he was selfish but food was food and if it tasted good, he would be there chomping away.

'I guess you could be right, but we'll never know,' as Jack shrugged his shoulders and walked back and sat on the edge of the bed that he was sharing with Oscar. Henratty then proceeded to divide the bread equally. In actual fact there were exactly enough slices for everyone to have two each. She buttered each slice and then smothered them with the delicious homemade strawberry jam and handed everyone an equal portion of the soft bread.

Jack could not believe how good the bread tasted, it was so fresh! It then dawned on him, *if there was no way out of this mine, then, where could the mine inhabitants possibly be getting the bread from?*

'Hey, wait a minute,' demanded Jack.

'What is it now? I hope this is not another one of your outlandish ideas,' protested Henratty.

'Have you all not realised, we're in a mine with supposedly no way out! So, where are they getting fresh bread from? The strawberries I can just about understand as we are underneath a strawberry field, but how does one explain the bread and butter. There's only one explanation that springs to my mind: they're getting it above ground, and that means there's a way out ...' proclaimed Jack.

'If that's the case, why would these animals want to live down here when they can all get out and go back to their hometowns?' asked Lyndi Lou.

'Jack, could be right – I smell a "rat" and I think Cooper and Nora know the answer. Did you not notice how they would constantly gaze at each other from time to time almost as if they were waiting for us to say something out of the ordinary, and why were they asking how much we knew about the mine? Also did you notice how all the other inhabitants told us how they ended up in the mine and seemed to have a good reason for wanting to live down here but Nora, Cooper and Alfonso said nothing, very odd indeed,' noted Henratty.

'Diamonds I think!' declared Jack, as he stood up proudly. He then started to sift through his army jacket pockets, as he whipped out his tiny metal detector and said, 'And I have the very tool that will prove I was right all along!'

All the other meerkats were now staring at Jack perplexed by what he had alleged, as on first inspection one would not have a clue what this gadget was; it was quite deceiving. Jack had managed to persuade Papa Brian to let him have the metal detector, as his father had only ever used it once and it really was no use to him, and now this little device could just be their saving grace, well in Jack's eyes.

Henratty, Lyndi Lou and Oscar were listening intently as Jack continued with his farfetched theory as they finished their slices of bread and strawberry juice, when suddenly the door burst open. Luckily, Jack's quick reflexes had enabled him to slip his metal detector back into his army jacket pocket literally seconds before Nancy the hedgehog entered the dormitory.

'Don't panic, it's only me, Nancy. I've just come to collect the trays. I hope you enjoyed your breakfast, it was all homemade!' Henratty and Jack looked suspiciously at each other, but did not say anything.

They could see that Alfonso was hovering outside the door, arching his neck high to ensure Nancy would not come to any harm. He was hissing again to try to instil fear into the meerkats to ensure that they did not do anything stupid, not that they would when they were outnumbered.

'So, Nancy, did you make the bread yourself then?' Jack quizzed.

'You know the answer to that; we have been given strict instructions not to talk to any of you, until Nora said so.'

'Is that in case you slip up and make it known that there is a way out of here. Well, you can save your breath, as we have already worked out there is definitely a way out. We know there is no way you could possibly have made that fresh bread down here and even if you gave us some plausible explanation, where would you get the ingredients from? No matter how hard you try to convince us, we're not buying it, so you can go back to the "old bat" and give her that message,' Jack retaliated assertively.

Upon hearing Jack's counter-attack, Alfonso raised his head above Nancy and moved much closer to him. He was almost touching his face, but Jack was fearless and did not budge an inch despite Alfonso's apparent intimidation.

'Listen, Jack, I suggest you watch that tongue of yours and show a little respect to Nancy, who incidentally was the one that managed to persuade Nora to give you all something to eat. She is the kindest, most hardworking and loyal hedgehog I know. So, if she said she made the bread *here*, then that's what she did. I suggest you think twice before you speak to Nancy like that again and thank your lucky stars it was not Nora you had just spoken to like that.'

'Look, Mr Rattlesnake Not! I'm not scared of you. No matter how threatening you get nothing will convince us that there is not a way out of here. Whatever reason you guys are down here, has nothing to do with us and to be honest, we really don't care. All we want to do is go home. Furthermore, whatever you are all hiding or guarding down here, is of no interest to us. It could be diamonds for all we care – we just want to go home, so go back to "Ms Bat" and relay what I have said, perhaps we could negotiate?' Jack suggested bravely.

Alfonso's head shot back in utter amazement. He could not believe someone as young as Jack could be so upfront and brash enough to challenge someone like Nora, whom everyone, although were scared of, respected for her wisdom and sincerity. She was harmless really but had such a presence one could not help feeling intimidated by her.

'Well, we'll see about that,' refuted Alfonso as he swiftly flicked his tail around and then said, 'Nancy, let's go.'

'I'll just grab the trays and I'm right behind you,' replied Nancy hesitantly. She then quickly went over to Jack, undetected by Alfonso who had now left the dormitory, and whispered, 'Look, Jack, if you want to get out of here in one piece, I suggest you don't speak anymore and keep your opinions to yourself, especially around Alfonso. You have been warned,' continued Nancy, as she shut the door behind her.

'Jack, have you gone completely mad ... now you've really done it?' shouted Henratty.

'Yes, not your finest moment,' said Oscar stating the obvious.

'I want mama, I want to go home, I hate it here and Jack is making everything worse,' sobbed Lyndi Lou. Everyone was staring at Jack stunned by what he had just alleged and were all waiting for an explanation.

'Oh, what now? Look, I'm convinced that Nora and Cooper are hiding something, something that the other inhabitants know nothing about, but something that they are convinced we know about. Am I making sense?'

'Can you repeat that again please, Jack,' requested Oscar.

'I think Nora, Cooper, Nancy, Jasper, Poppy, Escargot, with the exception of Enoch and possibly even Alfonso, are happy to live down here in this mine. Judging from the little bits they told us, they all have legitimate reasons for wanting to be here and seem quite happy and able to survive in this environment, whereas, Enoch is very forgetful and is not even sure why he's down here and something tells me that he wants to get out. If I'm right about the diamonds, Nora will want to interrogate us even more, especially as I insinuated that I knew about the diamonds, so I am going to pretend that I really do know that the diamonds exist and see how she reacts. If the bat starts to get flustered, then we have definitely stumbled onto something big! Somehow one of us is going to have to try to get out of here without being detected and I think I know how.'

Jack then explained that he had noticed whenever they lock the dormitory the meerkats were being kept in, they always leave the key in the door.

'So what's new – we've noticed that too?' retorted Henratty.

Jack was now holding the metal detector in the air and started waving it like a magic wand and grinning *like a Cheshire cat that had got the cream and more!*

'And what do I have here?'

'Oh, spit it out, Jack. We don't have time for your wisecracks!' demanded Henratty frustratingly.

'I'm sorry, well, this is not just any old metal detector, because it also has a magnet attached to it. When I press this button, the metal detector becomes magnetised so one can scoop up whatever treasure one finds underground especially when it's hard to get to.'

'So what if it's a magnet?'

'Do all of you really not understand what I have just said?

'Well, obviously not,' Henratty replied sarcastically.

'You see that gap underneath the door, I think my metal detector can just about reach under there, and if I extend the rod to say two feet and then activate the magnet, I reckon the force will be strong enough to rip that key out of its keyhole,' Jack deduced proudly.

'You're crazy!' asserted Henratty. 'Not a bad theory but I think you must be dreaming. Do you honestly think that it is going to work?'

'Absolutely, if you think you can do better, then please share your idea with us?' confronted Jack. Henratty now felt under extreme pressure as she racked her brains for a better solution, but nothing came to mind. The other meerkats looked on keenly awaiting her answer, but all she could do was shrug her shoulders with disappointment.

'I guess you've got me there, Jack. I really can't think of anything.'

'That's settled then! Later on tonight after Alfonso has done his final spot check, we will have the best window of opportunity and this is when I am going to attempt to grab that key. If successful, I will pop out, lock the door and replace the key, just in case they do another unexpected spot check so that everything will look normal and they do not become suspicious, as mark my words they will if they notice that key was missing.'

'Why can't we all go with you?' insisted Oscar.

'Because, firstly, unless we know exactly where we're going, this will undoubtedly slow us down especially as time is of the essence. However, if I go and check out the tunnels and try to find the direct route out of here, it will certainly save a lot of time, rather than us wandering aimlessly with no co-ordinates,' advised Jack.

'Are you going into battle mode again?' asked Oscar.

'Of course I am – this is definitely war this time ...'

'Reporting for duty, Sir,' Oscar said enthusiastically having complete faith in his brother. Jack was trying to make sure the two younger meerkats were not too frightened and if Oscar saw this as a *pretend* military procedure it would make him focus on the task at hand

and not be consumed by the possibility that none of them were getting out of here.

The door abruptly swung open again; this time it was just Alfonso.

'Come with me – Nora would like to see you, Jack, and you alone.' he ordered. *Was Jack's plan working? He had predicted that his outspoken words would cause a reaction and indeed they had, as now he alone was being summoned to seek counsel with Nora "The Great Bat".*

Jack was taken to the first dormitory on the other side of the base camp by Alfonso who insisted that Jack walked in front of him. It was clear that Alfonso did not trust him at all, but now was not the time for him to attack Alfonso; Jack had to think of the safety of Oscar and the other meerkats. He was now standing outside a dormitory, where the plaque above the wooden door said "Ms Nora". Alfonso opened the door and gave a nod for Jack to enter which he did promptly as the door slammed behind him. The first thing he noticed was that this dormitory was a lot smaller in comparison to the others he had seen.

Nora and Cooper were sitting around a wooden table with one spare seat which he assumed must be for him. There was a short pause and then Nora spoke.

'Please make yourself comfortable and help yourself to some strawberry juice and freshly baked scones made by our very own Nancy, *homemade* mind you!'

So Jack had touched a nerve, as she mentioned the word "homemade", which had been the subject of his confrontation with Alfonso, when he insinuated that the bread could not have been homemade and somehow came from above ground, which Alfonso ferociously refuted.

'Well, Jack, you sure do have an imaginative mind, if there was a way out of here don't you think we would have left here many years ago? Look around you, would anyone in their right mind want to live down here for all eternity?' construed Cooper.

'Maybe – who knows – whatever makes one happy.'

'A Smart Alec too!'

'What do you know about diamonds, as you seem to think we were sitting on a fortune down here?' asked Nora, as Cooper began to laugh.

Jack began to think that perhaps he was just fantasising and, after all, Nora was right, *who would want to stay down here really, especially if there was a way out?* But then he thought maybe the other inhabitants down here did realise there was a way out but just did not want to go, especially after what they had been through. Now he really was confused.

'Look Batty…'

'Only Enoch calls me Batty and he has good reason to, but I insist you call me Nora.'

'All right, Nora, maybe I'm wrong about the diamonds … I just said that on a whim to see if it would provoke a reaction. All we want to do is get out of here and we promise you we won't mention this place! We can just say we fell down the mine and eventually found our way out. All they will do is close the strawberry fields completely or ensure that the prohibited area above the mineshaft is well and truly fenced off so no one can ever again get in the position we were in. I'm sure once they know what happened to us, no one would dare to venture here anyway, scared of the same thing happening to them,' concocted Jack.

'So no more talk of diamonds then. The last thing we want is for Meerville Strawberry Fields to be the centre of attention and also that would mean Nancy, Jasper, Alfonso, Enoch, Poppy, Escargot and ourselves ending up homeless or even worse dead! Is that what you all want on your conscience? Also have you thought of the consequences for the inhabitants of Meerville? It would be like a circus up there what with all the media attention you would invoke with your wild story of diamonds,' insisted Nora.

'Does that mean you are now going to let us go, if we promise not to say anything?' Nora began to hoot as she let out this high pitched squawk and flapped her wings.

'Listen, no one's going anywhere, as I said to you there is no way out, so the best thing you can advise your little friends is that they better get used to their new home. Now, the choice is yours, we can either all live as one happy family or we can keep you locked up for as long as we decide to, until you all conform,' said Nora as she stared at Jack. Jack could not believe what the old bat was saying.

Nora then summoned Alfonso back into the dormitory, but little did she know that he had been eavesdropping on her conversation with Jack, something she would not be pleased with if she ever caught him in the act. Alfonso decided to wait a few seconds as he composed himself and then entered the dormitory. A suspicious glare from Nora did not go unnoticed as Alfonso slid into the room. Nora never missed a trick and deep down she always knew he would listen in on her conversations but she trusted him implicitly.

'Alfonso, take this rude little meerkat back to the dormitory and tell Nancy that our intruders are not to have any food for tonight, as punishment for his rebellious behaviour.'

'Mark my words, Batty, we will get out of here. I'm not scared of you and your cronies, especially that snake, and I will find a way out of here, you'll see!' Clearly Cooper had been angered by what he had just said and for the second time he was no longer in a stooped position.

'You sure do have a mouth on you, Jack. One day you will learn to keep your opinions to yourself, as all it does is get you in trouble. When will you ever learn?' On that note Jack was led away by Alfonso back to the dormitory.

CHAPTER TEN

A Way Out

Jack had arrived back in the dormitory as Henratty and the others breathed a sigh of relief, happy to see that he was still in one piece.

'What happened – are you all right?'

Jack had decided he was not going to tell them what Nora had conveyed about not getting out of the mine. He was even more convinced now there was a way out and that there were definitely diamonds down here, but how could he prove this. He must find a way out tonight and tonight only, otherwise they were doomed. Therefore, reluctantly he decided he would take Henratty with him – two heads were better than one and they could look out for each other. Oscar could take responsibility and look after Lyndi Lou, which Jack knew he would be happy to do and would take this command seriously.

There was no time to spare and he was determined not only to find a way out but prove, once and for all, that there were indeed diamonds in this disused mine and he was adamant that Nora and Cooper, the bat and the rat, knew they were down here. But Nora was also correct when she advised that if the media found out, Meerville Town would be like a circus – *Could Jack honestly risk inflicting this on his hometown?* He needed to believe he could get everyone out of here safely and hoped the MightyKats would answer his prayer.

He had gone into a trance-like state whilst contemplating how he was going to get everyone out of here. It wasn't until Henratty clicked her fingers in front of his face, did he snap out of his trance.

'Henratty, we have to get out of here as soon as possible, and I need you to come with me tonight to see if we can find a way out of this mine,' Jack blurted out.

'But what about Lyndi Lou and Oscar – we cannot leave them?' insisted Henratty.

'You have to trust me on this occasion, I am being deadly serious. The safest place at the moment is for them to stay here, they would only slow us down and we would probably end up getting caught. Also we need them to stay here just in case Alfonso does a spot check when we are out, at least then when he looks in our dormitory, everything will appear as normal. He will think there are four bodies altogether in those beds and we can use our pillows as decoys,' informed Jack.

'But we want to go with you,' pleaded Oscar.

'You know your big brother would never let you down nor leave you here. I need you to be brave and strong and look after Lyndi Lou. Can you do that for me? We will definitely come back for you both, that's a promise.' As Oscar gazed deeply into Jack's eyes, he actually knew his brother was being sincere but there was definitely something Jack was not telling him, Oscar knew his brother all too well, but now was not the time to question him. He paused for a brief moment, thinking carefully about his brother's every word but in the end he always did whatever his brother asked of him.

'I think I can do it ... I will pray to the MightyKats to protect all of us and get us out of here safely,' vowed Oscar.

'That's the spirit!' said Jack.

'And as for you, Lyndi Lou,' said Henratty, 'I need you also to be very brave and stay with Oscar. Do you understand?' Lyndi Lou looked frightened and nodded her head as she hugged her big sister.

'Right, Jack, that settles things. I'm ready when you are – we'll definitely go tonight then.'

While Lyndi Lou and Oscar were in the corner of the dormitory talking and keeping themselves amused, Henratty decided she would speak to Jack in private.

'Is there something you have not told me following your meeting with Nora and Cooper? I can tell that something has definitely alarmed you?' Jack thought, *deny, deny!* He knew Henratty was tough but he did not want to upset her.

'Don't be so silly, do I look like I'm scared of any of them? You know if I had had my own way, I would have pinned that snake down to the ground a long time ago. We can all see that he seems the most ferocious and the one to watch. I think the rest of them are harmless really, but that snake has a glint in his eyes; he's thirsting for blood and *our blood*. I just want to get out of here, more so for the sake of Oscar and Lyndi Lou; they look so fragile.'

'I agree, but you would tell me if something was wrong, wouldn't you, Jack?' questioned Henratty.

'Absolutely, Meerkats' Honour! We need to decide about the order of events for tonight: I noticed last night whilst you were all asleep that Alfonso does two spot checks at night, so after his final check, I suggest we give it a good fifteen to twenty minutes before I attempt to remove the key from the keyhole with my little device and then we'll set off. We can use the torch to search the tunnels.'

'But have you forgotten – the battery died?' recalled Henratty.

'Of course, I haven't. I forgot to mention that I found some spare batteries in the inside pocket of my army jacket,' informed Jack. Henratty could not believe their luck and jumped up and gave Jack a hug. He did not know what to do as she had never ever shown him such affection, but I guess she had good cause to be excited and grateful. Jack had promised that with his trusted torch he would get them all out of here and that is exactly what he was going to do.

'I suggest that we follow the tram tracks in the opposite direction to where we were picked up, therefore, we should turn left when we leave the main entrance of the dormitories. Something tells me these tram tracks are the means of a way out of here. There is just one rule we must obey, though,' conveyed Jack.

'And what might that be?'

'We cannot make a sound – that Nora was no fool and she had the most astounding hearing, I think she would hear a pin drop on the other side of the tunnel no matter how far away she was. I think we should hold hands along the tunnel, then if you need to show me something or get my attention just squeeze my hand tightly, Henratty, and I'll do the same, but let's hope we don't have to do that,' suggested Jack.

'Okay, I've got you loud and clear,' answered Henratty reassuringly.

'Secondly, if we do get caught and one of us was able to escape, I suggest whoever it was ran for their life and tried to find a way out. We must not fail, Oscar and Lyndi Lou are depending on us to not let them down,' reminded Jack.

'I agree. So, we'll wait until tonight. I strongly advise that we get some sleep to ensure we are fully alert later because we can't afford to make any mistakes,' stated Henratty.

* * *

Back in Nora's dormitory, Nora and Cooper were mulling over recent events, especially their little conversation with Jack.

'So, Nora, what do you think, does Jack know anything for sure about the diamonds or is he just bluffing?'

'I have to say he is not as dumb as he looks! I'm still not sure but I would say that he is pretty confident there are diamonds down here, even though he has no proof. I think we will definitely need to keep an eye on him.'

'But perhaps he meant what he said, that if we let them go and show them the way out, they won't say a word. I think what you said about the media frenzy sunk into that tiny brain of his and you could tell from his reaction that it struck a chord. I don't think he wants his or anybody else's home invaded by the media. You can tell he loves living in Meerville, as do all of us!' speculated Cooper.

'But can we take that risk? If the Larkans in Skylark get a hint of any mention of diamonds, we are all doomed. You know how precious those diamonds will be to the Larkans, their power would be phenomenal and I don't even think the MightyKats could stop them,' said Nora.

'You honestly believe these superheroes exist, don't you? Have you ever seen one?' asked Cooper intriguingly.

'No, but I have heard so many stories from reliable sources that were far too vivid for me not to believe. They say if you just call out to them or even think of them and ask for help, your prayers will be answered.'

'What a load of nonsense. If that were the case, why have they not come to rescue all of us and think of a way of defeating the Larkans?' proclaimed Cooper.

'The MightyKats only appear when we are in grave danger and when the Land of Arkvale is threatened with extinction (nature has to take its course). Also, we have not seen any activity from the Larkans, as they cannot yet pinpoint where the diamonds are, but it only takes something like this to get out to the media and they will have their answer,' alleged Nora.

CHAPTER ELEVEN

Alfonso The Snake Fake

All the inhabitants, apart from Nora, Cooper, and Nancy who had gone to fetch food above ground, were in Cooper's dormitory. Alfonso had just returned following Jack's visit to Nora and Cooper earlier this afternoon.

'So what did our new found friends say?' asked Enoch excitedly.

'They maybe your friends, but they are not mine, I prefer to use the word "enemies" – that Jack is very cunning and certainly does not know when to keep his mouth shut,' growled Alfonso. One could tell that he had certainly got under Alfonso's skin and if he had his way, Jack and his friends would probably be dead by now.

'Oh, Alfonso, why do you have to be so harsh? You always seem to be so much angrier when you have lost your rattle. I think you feel a little threatened by them, Jack in particular. He's quite an intuitive little meerkat despite his appearance, a bit like me!' remarked Enoch. Immediately, Jasper, Alfonso, Poppy and even Escargot, who had just made an appearance, began to giggle hysterically. Even though Escargot was sound asleep his antennae were fully active and would alert him to anything interesting that was being disclosed outside his little crustacean habitat.

'Well, what's so funny then, I've obviously missed the joke, as I'm the only one not laughing?'

'Oh, Enoch, you're so funny even when you're not trying to be funny and that's what we love about you. Don't pay us any mind, you know we're only larking about. It's just that you do say the most ironic things,' said Poppy.

'And what was so ironic about what I just said?' Poppy just did not have the heart to tell him that he was nothing like Jack, apart from having the same waistline!

'It will take too long for me to explain to you – it's not important – ask me when it's quieter, then I will tell you.' She hoped by then Enoch would have long forgotten, well, in fact, she knew by then he would have forgotten. She did not want to upset Enoch as he truly was the most loveable mole one could ever meet, albeit a bit daft sometimes.

'I'm inclined to agree with Alfonso, that Jack is the one to watch. He is the most outspoken and it's hard to say what the other meerkats were like. I would probably guess that the one with the red beret and cape, Henratty, seems pretty astute too. So, personally, I think we should tell Nora to keep an eye on both of them for now,' suggested Jasper.

'And let's not forget how clever Jack is – he certainly quick-witted enough to work out that the bread could not possibly have been homemade, and is now convinced that there is a way out,' noted Alfonso.

'But there isn't a way out?' disputed Enoch. 'Or is there?'

'Oh, Enoch, you know there's a way out and we are all free to leave whenever we want to, but we choose to stay as this mine is our home and has kept us safe and away from the real predators. Even you have left the mine but returned within hours, as you can't find your way back home and the dark up there scares you even more than being in the dark down here,' said Poppy.

'I guess you're right and besides you guys are family to me, I would be lost without you. How could I ever leave you?'

'So, our *petit amis* are giving Nora and Cooper a hard time, *Je suis regard*?' noted Escargot intriguingly. 'I wish I could have been there to see Cooper's face when they questioned Jack.'

'What for? You probably would not have stayed awake long enough!' bellowed Alfonso, as they all cackled once more, but this time the joke was on Escargot.

'Well, yes I like to sleep but, Alfonso, how many times have I caught you snoozing when on lookout and not mentioned a word to Nora, so I suggest you think twice before you make fun of me.' And on that note Escargot retracted his neck back into his shell in a huff as if to say, *I rest my case!* Everyone was now staring at Alfonso – his secret was out …

'Look, guys, I can explain.'

'Yes, why don't you explain,' scowled Jasper. It was mostly Jasper and Alfonso that took watch and every now and again Enoch would have to do a shift just so they both had a bit of a respite. However, unlike Alfonso, Jasper was always honourable and never fell asleep no matter how tired he was, as the welfare of his friends and his home was of the utmost importance.

Escargot's head popped out once again, he was revelling in this, as when Nora found out, Alfonso would no longer be "the golden snake" anymore, more like "Alfonso the snake fake" as he had well and truly been rumbled. Escargot was laughing hideously as his neck was now hyperextended out of his shell. Suddenly Alfonso raised his head way up high and shot over to Escargot, hissing venomously.

'Just you wait you slimy toe rag – one lick from me and you would be no more, but you can thank your lucky stars that I detest snails and would not touch or eat you if you were the last edible thing left on Arkvale – I'd rather die of starvation.'

'Then die you must, but the fact remains I told the truth about your sneaky ways. No wonder you think Jack is a snide, it obviously takes one to know one!' Alfonso's eyes widened as he raised his head once more and flicked it back in anticipation of a kill. Escargot had angered him so much that he was about to gobble him up in one swoop despite what he had just professed. However, luckily for Escargot, he was saved by the sudden presence of Nora and Cooper.

'Alfonso, what do you think you are doing? It's not our friends that you should be terrorising!'

'I'm sorry, Nora, but Escargot is spreading lies about me.'

'It's no lie, I speak the truth and nothing but the truth.'

'Look, we can deal with that later. At this moment in time, we should be concentrating on ensuring our intruders do not try to escape, as I suspect they know there was a way out of here. Speaking of which, Alfonso, shouldn't you have checked on our little visitors by now?'

'Yes, yes, Nora! I did not realise we had all been in here for so long,' as he slinked away. He had not finished with Escargot and would deal with him later for his betrayal of trust – he had promised Alfonso he would not say a word!

CHAPTER TWELVE

The Great Escape – Part One

'Now listen everyone, Alfonso should have been here by now – he's late,' remarked Jack. But only a few seconds had passed, when suddenly they heard movement outside the dormitory door. They immediately lay still in bed as if fast asleep so that Alfonso would think everything was normal. As the door opened with a creak, they could hear Alfonso gliding towards them. He was now hovering over Jack and hissing ...

'I'm watching you Jack, you maybe asleep but mark my words any attempt to escape, I vow to catch you and then you will be mine,' Alfonso sneered and then off he went as he locked the dormitory door securely.

'What was that about ... what did you do in that meeting?' questioned Henratty.

'Nothing, Alfonso has had it in for me from day one, that's all, he obviously feels threatened by me. It's nothing to worry about, one of his colleagues has probably rattled his cage and he needs to take it out on someone, that someone being me ... anyway, we'll all be out of here soon. Now listen, Oscar, we are going to leave shortly, as that visit in theory should have been the last inspection for the night, however, if he comes back, you know what to do. I can't imagine Alfonso will check that closely again; I think he would have calmed down after a little while. If he shows up again, just stay calm and pretend to sleep even if you were awake. Have you both got that?' Oscar and Lyndi Lou both nodded their heads timidly – they were very scared and Jack and Henratty knew it. They had to leave immediately or risk never getting out of this mine forever.

Jack flicked open the metal detector and shoved it under the dormitory door through the gap, luckily the lights were left on outside, so he could aim the metal detector rod towards the keyhole. Once in place, he activated the magnet on the metal detector and instantly the key was yanked out of the keyhole. He then retracted the rod and with the key still intact he pulled the metal detector rod back under the door.

'Well done, that was magnificent; I really did not expect you to get the key so quickly,' stated Henratty.

Jack then inserted the key quietly into the keyhole and gently turned it to unlock the door. He signalled to Henratty as if to say, *Are you ready?* They both took a deep breath and tiptoed out of the dormitory. He then placed the key back in the door locking Oscar and Lyndi Lou in, who could be seen making up the beds using the pillows to make it look like Henratty and Jack were still there and hoped they had done a good enough job to deceive Alfonso – only time would tell ...

Henratty and Jack tiptoed along the main hallway stealthy until they came to the big wooden door entrance, which miraculously was open, as if someone had gone out, *but who would be wandering around these tunnels at this time of the night?* they thought but this was not the time to speculate as they had a job to do. They turned left into the dark and dusty tunnel and began to follow the tram tracks, as Jack gripped Henratty's hand tightly. He had the torch at the ready in his other hand, but he was not going to use it until he was as far away from the dormitories as possible.

They had been walking for approximately twenty minutes, when suddenly Jack thought he heard something clinking further up the tunnel. He immediately squeezed Henratty's hand tightly as he sensed she may not have heard – he did after all have the best hearing. Suddenly, there was that clinking sound again, it seemed to be getting louder and louder and the sound was certainly coming from further up the tunnel but whatever it was, was coming their way. Luckily, he had felt along the walls and realised they had reached a junction where they could either stay on the same tunnel or turn left into another tunnel. Jack instantly turned left, tugging Henratty along with him. Immediately he pressed his body and Henratty's body with his right arm against the wall. Because the sound was so close it seemed like they only had seconds to spare, and indeed, as they craned their necks to the right, they were surprised to see Nancy walking past holding a lantern and pushing what appeared to be an old-fashioned wheelbarrow, which contained some bread, strawberries, eggs and a few other items that were not so visible:

Nancy had just got back from her regular weekly trip to Meerville Town Centre to stock up on their supplies. Her brother, Jasper, sometimes accompanied her depending on what they needed, but most of the time she went alone. It was only ever Nancy and Jasper who went outside to stock up on food, as being hedgehogs they could run for miles and Meerville Town Centre was six miles away, which meant they had to give themselves at least four hours to get there and back, undetected. They were in meerkat territory, and if a hedgehog was seen in this vicinity, it could cause serious problems for Picklesby, their hometown – every species in Arkvale was governed by strict laws regarding when they should and should not enter each others territory.

There was always fresh bread and eggs left outside the shops, and as Nora had advised wisely, it was always best to only ever take two loaves of bread at any given time; to take any more would arouse suspicion and this principle applied to whatever they took. However, they were allowed to take any food thrown out or left near the shop bins as usually they had gone past their "sell by date" but they were usually only just out of date and still edible. Obtaining fruits was more difficult and time consuming; strawberries were never a problem, after all they lived under a strawberry field and as long as they were in season they knew they had ample supply. Collecting other fruits, however, involved a much higher risk, as although they were left outside the shops these were usually picked up for disposal within the hour. Therefore, this task was done jointly by Nancy and Jasper and considering they had been doing this task for over two years now, so far they had managed to get away with things having only nearly got caught once and from this incident they had learnt that timing and speed were crucial to not getting caught!

So Jack was right, their food source was, indeed, above ground, which meant there was also definitely a way out and they knew it had to be in the direction Nancy was coming from. They waited a few more minutes and then continued along the tunnel they were initially on. As they turned the bend, Jack decided he would use his torch as they were slowly running out of time and they needed to get back to that dormitory fast. They quickened their pace and knew as long as they could hear the wheelbarrow clanging, their movements would be distorted and Nora would be unable to detect them. But, unbeknown to Jack, she only used her echolocation *when necessary*, otherwise she would not get any peace or more importantly any sleep. Having exceptional hearing also had its drawbacks and Nora certainly needed to sleep just like anybody else.

* * *

After walking for another ten minutes, they suddenly came to a dead end, but how could this be? Jack then let go of Henratty's hand and started to feel the wall, and as he tapped on it, he knew that this was a false wall; it sounded hollow. He continued to feel around when his hand got caught on something sticking out of the wall. He switched the torch on for a few seconds and noticed a lever which he pulled on. Immediately the wall began to open up in a sliding motion and there before them was the mineshaft lift. *Very clever* – it had been hidden to appear as if it was part of the tunnel. He quickly pulled the lever once more to close the lift, and then grabbed Henratty's hand as they began to make their way back to their dormitory.

By the time they got back to the tunnel junction, Nancy had just entered base camp where Jasper greeted her.

'Any problems, Nancy?'

'None at all! In fact, it gets easier every time I do this. So, Jasper, tell me what I've missed,' as she handed him the wheelbarrow and they made their way to the dormitory marked "Stock Room" on the left.

CHAPTER THIRTEEN

The Great Escape – Part Two

Jack and Henratty were back at the main entrance of the dormitories. The door was not as ajar as it had been before, which meant visibility into the hallway leading to their dormitory was massively reduced, but they had to risk it before the next possible spot check.

As they entered the hallway, they could hear voices coming from the end dormitory along with the sound of bottles, tins and bags being moved around. Jack decided to sprint to their dormitory, quickly followed by Henratty. He slowly opened the dormitory door, leaving the key in the door without locking it as they slipped inside where they found Oscar and Lyndi Lou asleep. Henratty quickly whispered to them to get up, as they were now ready for the second phase of their plan and that was to get out of this mine, having found the mine-shaft lift. They quickly assembled all four pillows to make it look like they were asleep, and one by one Jack signalled for them to tiptoe out of the dormitory. He then quickly left a teasing note under the covers which he knew would infuriate Alfonso even more, but he felt he deserved it.

Jack was just about to leave the dormitory when luckily he heard Jasper coming down the hallway, but, miraculously, Nancy shouted at Jasper, to come back quickly, as Jasper sprinted to the stock room.

Jack was perspiring heavily, his hands were clammy and he was shaking a little. He opened the door swiftly and with nerves of steel, he quickly locked the door and sprinted for the main entrance. He did not care if he made a sound as Nancy and Jasper were making more of a racket in the stock room. Nancy had accidentally dropped a big jar of pickles that had gone everywhere and the whole room was splattered with vinegar so she needed help wiping up the mess before it ruined all the groceries.

'Oh, Nancy, how many times have I told you to leave this to me?'

'I know Jasper, but you know I always try and do things for myself.'

'Well, try to remember that your brother does not mind helping you, so next time ask!' ordered Jasper.

'You're the boss and yes you're right, I'll ask next time. It will certainly save me or rather us all this grief,' as they began to laugh at Nancy's stupidity. Before they knew it, most of the other inhabitants were now standing in the stock room with them. As they looked around, Nora had just walked in followed by Cooper.

'Are you two all right? We thought that maybe you had got into a spot of bother with our little guests?'

'Oh, sorry, Nora! I spilt a big jar of pickles and it has made a bit of a mess but we'll clear it up – nothing to do with our guests at all, they're locked up safely and are certainly not going anywhere.' On that note Alfonso thought as he was up, he might as well check on the meerkats, *only* because he wanted to tease Jack a little more.

As Alfonso opened the meerkats' dormitory door, with more visibility as the main dormitory lights were fully on, he instantly noticed there was something strange about the two beds. He moved in quickly and pulled back the covers of Henratty's and Lyndi Lou's bed only to find the two pillows. With even more haste, he flicked back Jack's and Oscar's covers but this time there were not just two pillows but Jack's note, which read:

Goodbye, Alfonso! You little hissy sissy. Let's see how you are going to explain this one to Nora. This time it will be you that's "rattling" with fear when she takes your head off ... The next time you threaten me or my friends, I will not only hit you right between the eyes but I will ensure you can never rattle again, Mr Snake! Well, let's say Nora will make sure of that!

Alfonso's eyes widened in fury and his whole body was now raging with so much anger.

He quickly glided back to the stock room.

'Nora, everyone, OUR PRISONERS HAVE ESCAPED!' wailed Alfonso. He was shaking a little in fear of what Nora would do to him.

'What do you mean, they've escaped? Did you not check the dormitory when I told you to?'

'Of course I did,' rebuffed Alfonso. However, from the look on everyone else's faces, it left much speculation, especially as Escargot had mentioned earlier how Alfonso would just sleep on lookouts!

'I swear to you, Nora, I checked that dormitory and they were all there and I locked up afterwards. Besides, the key was still locked in the door, so maybe someone can explain how they got out, or just maybe someone let them out?' This accusation caused even more outrage with the other inhabitants who all gasped in horror.

'How could you say that?' refuted Enoch.

'Maybe it was you, Enoch,' suggested Alfonso.

'I have to disagree,' retorted Poppy, 'Enoch has been with me the whole time, and I think everyone can account for their whereabouts except for you, Alfonso.' Nora then interrupted the somewhat heated debate.

'Look, this is not the time for in-house squabbling, we need to find those meerkats and find them fast! If they get out of here we are doomed ... do you hear me DOOMED... Alfonso and Jasper, please check the dormitory once more to see if they escaped directly from there. Could they have dug their way out, so check under the beds, but I doubt that very much. Now, Enoch and Nancy I suggest you start searching the tunnel in the direction we trapped them in the first place, whilst Cooper and I will go and get the tram and head towards the mineshaft lift just in case they have worked out where it was. Nancy, could they have heard you and Jasper discussing the lift at any stage?' asked Nora anxiously.

'Absolutely not, this is one thing we can guarantee; we have never mentioned the mineshaft lift at any time. It's the one code of conduct we have obeyed ... one hundred percent!'

'Right that settles it, we all know what we have to do. My echolocation should be able to pick them up in no time, as one thing in our favour is that they still don't know where the mineshaft lift is located, but little did Nora know that was not the case. She then clapped her hands continuously ...

'Now let's get going – time is of the essence – WE MUST NOT FAIL!' grumbled Nora.

Whilst Jasper double checked the meerkats' dormitory, Alfonso had automatically made a head start for the mineshaft.

* * *

The meerkats had now reached that familiar junction where they stopped for a moment.

'Listen, what's that? Oh, no it's the tram – they've obviously realised we've escaped. Now I don't care if they can see us,' as Jack got his torch out and shone it down the tunnel.

'Run! Run! RUN!' he bellowed, and indeed they started running, but what they did not realise was that Jack was no longer behind them. He knew that if they were to stand a chance of escaping, he would have to create some kind of diversion. He turned around and was now shining the torch in the opposite direction – *yes* towards the tram.

Further up the tunnel, Alfonso could see the blinding torch as he was not that far away from Jack. He began to hiss, ready for the kill, but Jack was waiting for him and was by this time crouched on the ground still aiming the torch down the tunnel. He quickly got out his binoculars, which he had set to infra-red mode. *At last, there's Mr Snake!* He then set his catapult with the biggest stone he could find. He had one chance and one chance only to knock Alfonso out. He was going to hit him straight between his eyes, just as his note had conveyed. Alfonso was only five yards away from Jack – as he got nearer to the junction, his hissing was louder than ever – he knew he was about to make his kill. Four yards, three yards and now two yards away, and so their eyes met. *Why was Jack skulking so low?* he wondered. Too late ... one yard away as Jack raised his head and released the catapult as the stone caught Alfonso right between the eyes. He did not know what had hit him, as his head jolted backwards then forwards, as he slumped to the ground with a loud thud and then slid forward only inches away from Jack.

Alfonso lay unconscious as Jack nudged him with his foot to make sure he was, in fact, out cold. He knew that snakes were very good at laying still and a prod like that would certainly have woken him up. Feeling sure Alfonso was unconscious, he began the fastest sprint for his life towards the mineshaft lift.

The other meerkats had now reached the mineshaft lift. Henratty desperately felt around the false wall looking for the lever to open the lift door, as Jack had done.

'Jack, help me,' she begged, but when her plea was not returned, they all realised he was not there.

'Where's, Jack?' yelled Oscar.

'I don't know,' as Henratty found the lever and pulled it down, 'But I do know we are not leaving without him.' The rusted mineshaft lift door flew open as she ushered Lyndi Lou and Oscar into the lift. Her hand was poised over the button to close the lift door, as they waited nervously.

Jasper had now found Alfonso, who was still out for the count. He began to shake Alfonso quite forcibly as he came to.

'Okay, Jasper, I'm awake now,' Alfonso groaned. He was still a little groggy and had a thumping headache. He was seeing stars but at least he was alive. 'That little

Jack stoned me and he is going to pay – mark my words,'
he seethed.

The tram had now pulled up as the brakes squeaked
loudly.

'Get in! GET IN!' Nora barked. She was Mad … Mad
… MAD! She cranked up the tram again and off they
sped in top gear.

Back in the lift, Henratty could hear Jack shouting –
his words were a little distorted, however, she could just
about make out what he had communicated, '*Get
everyone in the lift …*' At the same time, she could also
hear the tram closing in fast.

Sparks were flying from the wheels of the tram as it
was approaching Jack. He could feel that his legs were
wobbling like jelly, but he would not give in when he
was so close to getting out of this mine. With his last
bit of energy, he increased his speed, not knowing
where he had got his inner strength from, but he was
praying to the MightyKats as he was running – perhaps
it was working – they were somehow giving him the
inner strength to reach that lift which he could now
vaguely see between the misty hot air. He wiped the
sweat from his brow and continued in his stride. The
light in the lift was now visible, only thirty more yards
and he was "home".

Meanwhile, the wheels of the tram were red hot and
burning due to the intense speed and friction. The
wooden tram had now started to glow with flames, as
Jasper made an attempt to combat the fire with Cooper's
blanket.

'There's the little whippersnapper! We're nearly
there,' snarled Nora. The tram was only yards away
from Jack and closing.

Only ten yards to go, as Jack looked behind him just to see how close the tram was – it was gaining speed with every second.

'HENRATTY! ARE YOU READY, I'M HERE?' he shouted.

Through the mist, she was able to assess the situation pretty well. She told Oscar and Lyndi Lou to move out of the way and stay back in the corner of the lift. Suddenly she saw Jack do an enormous vault towards the lift, as she pressed the button. The doors were closing quickly when, by a split second, he slammed into the back of the lift as he slid to the ground and the doors shut solid behind him. The lift shook a bit but began to ascend slowly as it made its way out of the mineshaft as they all hugged Jack, who was sprawled out on the lift floor trying to catch his breath.

'Hey, take it easy everyone ...' Oscar and Lyndi Lou had now stopped hugging Jack, as Henratty peered over and gave him a kiss on the cheek. He froze in total shock as he touched the side of his cheek that she had just kissed.

'This is one day in my life that I won't forget ... I don't suppose you could do that again,' quipped Jack. Henratty had now composed herself. *What on earth was she thinking,* as she came to her senses! This time she looked down at Jack, her eyes flickered as if she was seriously going to kiss him on the cheek again, but instead she poked him in the stomach.

'You have got to be kidding, that is the first and last kiss you will ever get from me, so don't be having any more ideas! I simply got carried away with myself and that was me thanking you for saving our lives, especially when it was mostly my fault that we were down here in the first place.'

'MOSTLY?' proclaimed Jack.

'Okay, Jack, I shall rephrase that to COMPLETELY MY FAULT,' as everyone laughed and cheered, so relieved they were on their way out of the mineshaft and more importantly in one piece.

CHAPTER FOURTEEN

The MightyKats

Down in the mineshaft, Nora, Cooper, Alfonso and Jasper could only look on in disbelief as the lift continued to rattle its way to the top, as bits of dust began to fall on them. There was nothing more they could do as they turned and walked back towards the tram.

'So what now, Nora?' said Cooper.

'Nothing,' she responded calmly.

'But aren't you worried that those meerkats will come back for us?' asked Cooper.

'No, not at all, firstly because I think our little pep talk with Jack made him realise it would prove disastrous, not only for Meerville but Arkvale too, if the media knew about this place. He might be a risk taker but one could tell he was very astute and a calculated risk taker and somewhere inside that brain of his saw "reason". He loved his hometown and would do anything to ensure that it was protected. I'm sure he will think of a reasonable excuse as to why they went missing. Secondly, none of them ultimately want to get in trouble for entering the forbidden strawberry field.'

'But how can you be so sure?' asked Cooper.

'I'm sure, just trust me as you have always done.' Nora seemed pretty confident about this, as unlike the other inhabitants, Nora was able to detect the presence of a MightyKat who had entered the mineshaft immediately before the lift made its ascent. She knew then that everything would be taken care of and the mine would be safe once more. From the description that Nora had been given through various sightings by her ancestors and others, she knew the MightyKat she had just glimpsed was Cairo, and his special gift was the ability to not only read minds, but erase memories too. She knew the meerkats would not remember a thing in relation to recent events and there would be no mention of this mine, just an innocent day out strawberry picking with no recollection of what occurred on their second day out.

* * *

The mineshaft lift at last came to a halt, as the meerkats took a deep breath. They were so glad to embrace the cool fresh air; it had never felt or smelt so good. They dusted themselves off yet again, taking care to retrace their steps back out of the dangerous strawberry fields. Luckily it was still light enough to see, but darkness was fast approaching.

Once out of that field they climbed over the locked gates and walked briskly back to the Brians' house. They started talking about how many strawberries they had collected until they realised they had forgotten their baskets, but they were completely baffled as they could not understand how or why this had happened. They were now gawping at each other hoping one of them had the answer, but all that followed was complete silence, and then came the gust of wind. They continued the walk back home. They were now speechless, in a transient state fully absorbed in their own thoughts about their day out strawberry picking. The only problem was that none of them could recollect anything and more importantly, how were they going to explain the "inexplicable" to their parents!

* * *

An hour later, they had reached the Brian's house, as Mama Katie breathed a big sigh of relief and quickly rang Mama Mortimer to let her know that Henratty and Lyndi Lou had returned safely together with Jack and Oscar.

'And what time do you call this, Jack, and I'm talking to you as well, Henratty?' demanded Mama Katie sternly.

'What's the time mama ... we're not that late surely ... I honestly don't think we have been gone that long,' proclaimed Jack.

'I wouldn't say eight o'clock was early – would you?' Mama Katie could tell that they were all in genuine shock and could see that they just lost track of time, but even Henratty and Jack could not work out how they could have been playing for so long. Jack was even more puzzled by the time on the hallway clock, as his watch clearly said *ten o'clock*, but Mama Katie continued speaking before he could even say anything – he had so many unanswered questions.

'This time, Jack, don't even bother with your excuses, I don't want to hear any. All I can say is that you're both grounded for two weeks and I am sure the same will apply to Henratty and Lyndi Lou. I can see you've obviously all eaten the strawberries, so no more strawberry picking as that was clearly a waste of time,' noted Mama Katie.

They all stared at each other so surprised as they had not even realised they had been out that long, and well, yes, they did get locked in and had to climb the fence, but surely they had not been strawberry picking for most of the day. They just couldn't remember anything from the moment they entered that field.

'But we were only strawberry picking …' professed Oscar innocently, as Mama Katie stared at them suspiciously. She could see their clothes were grubby from being out for so long, but they had returned safely and once they had been given a stiff talking to, she was quite sure they would never be that late ever again, especially Jack! He just loved the great outdoors far too much to risk being grounded again for so long.

* * *

Papa Mortimer had just arrived to pick up Henratty and Lyndi Lou. They said their goodbyes and Jack and Oscar then went upstairs to get ready for bed.

Whilst Oscar was in the bathroom, Jack began to unload the gadgets from his army jacket, but as he got to his metal detector, he could see something shimmering that was wedged in the groove of the metal detector where the magnetised rod was extended from. *What was that,* he thought as he looked more closely at the gadget. *A diamond …Where did that come from?*

He then prised the little stone off the rod, looking somewhat surprised but pleasantly so. *'At last, I told papa there were diamonds on his land,'* Jack said to himself, but he decided he would not say anything to anyone, not even Oscar! Well, not just yet, as firstly he needed to find the exact location of the diamonds – the last thing Papa Brian wanted was loads of potholes on his land. He flicked the diamond up in the air, caught it and placed it among his other precious stones that he had collected in his treasure box. Jack was now ready for his next adventure: in his mind he had decided to call it *The Meerville Treasure Hunt,* as he grinned to himself.

* * *

Cairo had just returned to the MightyKats' base, Meer Space Station. He affirmed to his leader, Zammo, that "Mission Strawberry Fields" had been accomplished. He had not only erased the memories of the Brians' and Mortimers', but all the other meerkats' memories in Meerville Town that had any knowledge of the recent events. He had also adjusted the clocks at the households of the Brians' and Mortimers' to make it seem like Jack, Oscar, Henratty and Lyndi Lou had arrived home earlier than the actual time they had in fact arrived, which was, indeed, ten o'clock, as Jack had cleverly observed. Once they were all asleep, he would go back and amend the clocks with the correct time and no one would be the wiser, not even Jack!

The MightyKats were all looking at the screen into Jack's bedroom, as they smiled knowing he would keep his little treasure a secret until he discovered the exact whereabouts of the diamonds, a location he would never find, as he would be searching in the wrong place. The one thing the MightyKats were certain of, was that there were no diamonds on Papa Brian's land and the possibility of those meerkats ending up in that mineshaft ever again was zilch!

Zammo switched the screen off knowing The Land of Arkvale was safe again from those vultures, The Larkans of Skylark, and set the station to hibernate mode as the MightyKats retired once more in anticipation of their next mission …

Lightning Source UK Ltd.
Milton Keynes UK
UKOW04f2343030315

247238UK00001B/39/P